Wandering Roots
A Quabbin Quills Anthology

Perpetual Imagination
Boston • Northampton • New York

881 Main St #10
Fitchburg, MA 01420

info@perpetualimagination.com

Production Copyright © 2024
Quabbin Quills and Perpetual Imagination

Manufactured in The United States of America.

1 2 3 4 5 6 7 8 9 10

First Edition

ISBN-13: 978-1-7352576-4-8

Library of Congress Control Number in process for this title.

CONTENTS

SEVERED ROOTS

WANDERING ROOTS

2024 SCHOLARSHIP WINNERS

1ST PLACE WINNER

FORGOTTEN
Moss Maloney

If roots hold memories,

Then the ones of you

Must have rotted.

For even as I close my eyes,
Your face blurs into paste,
A concoction wasted away,
The face I used to see,

Now withering.

Smiles dripping onto tiled floor,
Pooling together into what
Might have been you,

Then the roots take over,
Locking away your memory

Where I could never reach.

2ND PLACE WINNER

THE PRETTY LADY AND THE WANDERING BIRD
Via Rose

The sun peeked through the blinds, like when you used to wake me up,
showing me I survived another day.
If it wasn't for you, I could lay in bed forever.
I'm not mad though, you make tomorrow feel like just another day.
You heard me, trusted me, and my poems felt deeper.

Because of you, I felt a connection,
like roots holding me in place in the shaking ground.
Without you, I felt like a soft feather, lost, drifting away in the sky,
a victim of the wind, everyone falling in front of me.
I didn't know what I had or what I was.

My thumb and finger reach for a pencil, my hand clenching a slice of dead life.
Deeper and deeper my fingers go, shifting and turning.
It's a mess, blowing away dust as time escapes every particle I write.
The roots that brought us together are now crushed, so I could write meaningless words
I know you'll never see.

The words I wanted to say SCREAM till my chest painfully vibrates.
 My pencil tests me, makes me think I don't know my own words but I know my emotion resonates in my own heart. That's all that matters.

In the dead of night, walking as one street lamp fills the park with light,
I bathe under the shine of the present air.
The street light flickers twice. I jump.
I look forward, seeing a pretty lady on the end of the park bench.

She's watching a tree dance, thriving, smiling, the glowing tendrils of her hair
bathing under the streetlight.
I can tell she is a wise woman, all I ever wanted to be.
I search, and it fails me.
I sit next to the pretty lady, a true legend that remains.
I turn to meet her endless gaze.
I try to release my words for the first time, but she says,

"I have lived through all, which equals nothing. There is no meaning.
We worry about the future, but really we're scared of repeating the past.
I am not a legend, I am just the roots connecting me to my true self."
She stands and inches towards the streetlight fog.
I hope that when the wind blows,
I fall as gently as a feather once more and get caught in the hands of the Pretty
Lady.

My ears catch the scattering sounds of an injured bird that has fallen from the
tree.
On repeat, I imagine a lost soul looking out, falling,
the thud stopping the endless cacophony, and outside view.
The roots betrayed him by letting him slip from stability.

I search, scanning to find the source, aware of my own symptoms:
irregular heartbeat, shortness of breath, chest pain? dizziness?
This is twice now that I felt a scream of agony, my skin paling,
vomit rising in my mouth.
There is no other explanation, a mere coincidence of the impossible.
I don't know how much of this screaming I can take.

I listen helplessly.
I think of you. Why is the screaming even louder than before?
I see a rush of blood beneath a purple sea, an exposition of rolling clouds,
and endless uneasiness.
Its wings, its source to fly, is a mess, the seeping blood turning crimson.
Disgusting.
How could I allow myself to freeze when time kept moving?

My mistake lingers, stabbing my muscles, like the tree root
being ripped from the ground in a storm. It was me.
The bird got quiet, but the air caused my lungs to scream.
The foundation gives in, my body collapses at the sight of the bird,
hoping for an indication of movement or at least a moving shadow.
I hyperventilate. The images won't go away,
driving me to believe there was something I could have done for you.

The streetlight flickers, the bird twitches,
teasing me, matching the pounding of my heart.
A feeling of understanding, I laugh. I touch his wing.
The twitching stops, the flickering stops.

He's there, with the sound of the night and drop of my pencil,
another example of the roots dying. I breathe,
a gust of wind makes it so my eyes can no longer see.
I can't see you anymore, are you talking?
Are you this poem on the flattened roots, where the birds once sang.

I see a life I'll never know, never understand.
Why did it have to be this way?
My legs finally take control, but so do the bird's wings.
The world around me gets lost in my relief.
Suddenly a flutter waves in the blink of an eye.
The outcome changes.
Not only for the bird, but I find strength in the moon that seeps upon me, my only love.
With a last flick of the streetlight, my pencil, my choices,
behold bad times that come to an end.
For the first time I am aware of the enticing beauty of the streetlight.
It flickers and then stops.

I am no longer afraid of the dark.

3RD PLACE WINNER
MY ROOTS GROW IN DIFFERENT
DIRECTIONS

Kassandra Santos

My roots grew in different directions.

But the most important thing to remember

When you feel scattered

Is that it's all attached within you.

And you may feel disoriented

But there is always a place to come back to:

A sense of home that lives in your heart.

The soil running through your body

Connects each part of yourself,

Whether they are dead or invasive roots.

My hands are covered in dirt

From burying the parts of me that are broke,

But they are cleaned by the water

From taking care of new seeds

That are planted to rebuild

What I lost in the drought

Of lacking the love I held for myself.

HONORABLE MENTION
MY JOURNEY
Alexander Murdock

My journey started many years ago,

When times were simpler and the world a little easier.

I came across a sudden break in my peace,

A break I would never forgive nor forget.

I was forced to leave home to start a new journey,

Feeling like a jeep traveling the bumpy desert.

Some moments were hard to bear and others had me in despair.

But now I've returned, to the place that gave me my start,

A place that allowed me to really see the evolution of my

character.

But I shall never forget what it really was: my journey.

HONORABLE MENTION

OLD ROOTS
Jayden Lindsay

Old roots connect us to everything from our past
Old friends, family, old places we have lived
Even people who made an impact on your life, but were only in
your life for a short time
Whether it be good or bad
The roots age as our relationships are tested
I had a friend once
Strong, young roots connected us
Then she began to try and hide behind the old, withered roots
She knows who she is
She isn't worth being called out by name

RELENTLESS
Jayden Lindsay

Black roots, twisting swirling, growing in any direction they
wanted
They snake across the ground, holding onto things
Things the wild winds weren't allowed to have
They dove underground, seeking nutrients and food
Some grew mushrooms, others grew moss
Some grew nothing at all
They seldom reached towards the sky, knowing it would not
welcome them happily
The sky threw wild winds at them, angrily attacking relentlessly as
the roots only grew stronger
They wanted the roots gone, they were old and past their prime
They couldn't be allowed
They wouldn't be allowed
Everyday the sky relentlessly attacked, but the roots never seemed
to weaken
They stood strongly against the wild winds
Everyday they were in their spots, strong in their posture and skills
They never gave up hope, as we shouldn't
We are like the roots
We stand for what we believe and we stand strong
We don't let others tear us down for our beliefs
We are the roots
Standing relentlessly against the sky as it attacks us
Never relenting until one dies

WAITING

Jayden Lindsay

In the forest waits
The roots of past people
Waiting to rise again
Waiting to restore their former glory
Waiting for the person who will set them free
Waiting to spread their roots across the globe
Waiting
Waiting
Waiting
Waiting for someone never to come
Waiting for the chosen who was killed to come
Waiting for their kin to come instead
Waiting for the right time to send their signal
Waiting for the perfect time
Waiting for the best opportunity
Waiting for the chosen to come forward
Waiting for them to finish the quest started by the first chosen
Millenia of waiting it seems
Waiting for the day that never comes
Waiting for the persons that never come
Waiting
Waiting
Waiting
Waiting no more
Accepting the time they wasted waiting
Accepting their close friend lied and isn't coming
Accepting they are alone in their journey
Accepting the waiting roots are me
Waiting for the perfect friend to come along

Roots Run Deep

"THE OLD SAW MILL"
WILLIAM BELISLE

THE LOST TOWNS BEEKEEPERS CLUB
Jim Metcalf

"Good afternoon, friends. Can our monthly meeting of the LTB come to order? This being our Christmas meeting, can we dispense with any business so we can enjoy our potluck holiday meal?"

A hand goes up in the audience. "Before we eat, I would like to report on a run-in with the law."

"Doctor Maloney, you have the floor, but make it quick as the food is getting cold."

"Thank you, Ralph," Doc Maloney stood in a formidable stance. "The snow and cold weather are worrying all of us, so on my way home from the hospital, I decided to check my hives. I walked around the edge of the snow-filled Hardwick field to my hives to listen for activity in each box. Since it was windy, I took my stethoscope out of my pocket and listened to each hive. All sounded strong, so I headed back to my car, only to be met by flashing blue lights and the sheriff at the gate," he said while waving his hands in effect. "He told me he got a call from someone driving by and reporting that they witnessed a crazy person with a stethoscope listening to piles of boxes on the far side of the field. The sheriff knows me but wanted to know if I had been drinking."

The audience broke out in an uproar of laughter, and then Bill Foster suggested, "Old Doc Maloney may have sniffed too much anesthesia."

Doc Maloney replied, "The next time you come in for an operation, Bill, I will use bee stings instead of anesthesia on you."

Jim Jackson yelled, "Where could I buy a stethoscope so I could aggravate people, as well?"

Ralph, the club president, quickly gaveled the meeting back to order, saying, "Let's eat."

This group of beekeepers was displaced from the five towns in the Swift River Valley when Boston decided to clear-cut forests, demolish homes, and move family graves to a new cemetery. Like almost everyone in the valley, they despised these destructive efforts, which tore their very roots from the ground and tossed them to the wind.

The beekeepers of the Swift River Valley were mainly farmers and close friends who helped each other throughout the seasons, attended church together, and even had children who kept the bonds strong through marriage. Everyone had to find new homes, farms, and ways to earn a living. But they stayed rooted in the Lost Towns Beekeepers Club.

Ralph, the club president, sat at the head of the table and smiled with pride. "We are few, but we have stayed close," he said.

"Yes," Doc Maloney agreed. "We assisted each other in finding farms for sale, open land, or alternative businesses and jobs that kept us close."

"It wasn't easy work," another beekeeper chimed in. "We were all paid next to nothing for our valley farms, while the properties we tried to buy were costly."

A couple of things kept these farmers together and focused on landing on their feet. It may have happened by accident, but practical jokes became a part of every meeting to keep spirits up and off their problems. Despite their constant ribbing, their roots intertwined with a sincere love for each other. While trying to find new homes close by and build a future, they often met to keep their spirits up, and they invited others to join them for Saturday afternoon potluck picnics. The talk was always about crops, livestock, and honeybees.

On one Saturday meeting at the Hoyt's, Barbara, the farmer's wife, announced, "I am the keeper of our bees, so if anyone wants to examine how well the hives were doing, I would be happy to open them for inspection." Since most men of that time felt beekeeping was a male activity, they winked at each other while gathering around the beehives, ready to expose her inadequate beekeeping skills. Barbara marched through a parting of the male circle carrying a baseball bat to the hives.

One farmer yelled, "Did you forget your smoker, Miss?"

Barbara replied, "Smoking the hives causes lung problems for the bees, so I quiet them down with noise."

As the snickers began, Barbara took a Red Sox batter's stance and proceeded to bang loudly on the hive cover with the bat. With the first bang on the hive, all the men started screaming and running over each other to reach the safety of their truck cabs. Barbara was beside herself in laughter.

Apparently, she had placed a stack of empty hive boxes among her live hives. The men assumed the boxes were full of bees and the banging would bring forth clouds of angry bees. A hearty cheer was heard from the wives at the picnic table. The story about the woman who put a group of screaming male beekeepers in their trucks never got old. As a result, Barbara started something, and beekeepers began to think up practical jokes for their turn at hosting a Saturday afternoon picnic.

But at the next beekeeper's picnic, the hosting farmer and his wife, Mary and Jim Hanson, were quiet, elderly apple growers and church leaders. Hence, everyone expected delicious pies but no practical jokes. Nevertheless, since hive openings for inspection and teaching became the start of the gatherings, the now cautious beekeepers gathered in a wider circle than at the Hoyt's to see how these bees were doing.

A new first-year beekeeper asked if he could smoke the hive for opening. He was given the smoker and nervously began to rapidly pump the bellows, creating clouds of choking smoke, causing everyone to choke and gag. As he blew the dense smoke into the hive opening, a loud alarm began to sound, "Whoop! Whoop! Whoop!" It was followed by the announcement, "Leave the building immediately! Leave the building immediately!"

The old couple hosting the gathering grabbed each other in fall-down laughter. The owners had inserted one of those new-fangled fire alarms in the hive.

Practical jokes, stories, and laughter resulted in friendships that began to build a club-like atmosphere where people wanted to continue meeting throughout the winter. Potluck suppers continued, and new neighbors started to ask about learning how to keep honeybees. Little by little, this group of displaced farmers began to plant roots in their new communities while holding on to the friendships of the valley they left.

At some point, Ralph asked, "Could we make our group officially a club? Maybe we can call ourselves the lost towns beekeepers." About eight or ten people shouted, "Second." And The Lost Towns Beekeepers Club bloomed from what began as a tragedy. People wanted to join this family of happy, fun-loving beekeepers to learn more about this hobby, so an annual beekeeping class began. The old-timers gained respect as teachers but not without their love for practical jokes.

During the late winter and early spring, weekly classes began at the Methodist Church Hall. The old beekeepers led the classes covering all aspects of keeping honey bees, from building equipment to examining hives for disease to harvesting honey and wax—of course, with humor included.

Harold Scates, a pig farmer, welcomed a new class with the announcement, "Your relatives and neighbors are going to think you're crazy, so I'm going to tell you new beekeepers how to impress them." Harold asked, "Would you like to teach your honeybees how to read?"

A skeptical "Yes" was heard from the students.

Harold went on to say, "If you observe the hive's entrance, you will notice that the bees enter and exit the hive on opposite sides of the opening to avoid collisions. Then, to impress friends, tack up two small signs that say ENTER and EXIT over the appropriate side of the hive entrance and show your friends that you had taught the bees to read."

"How about calling your bees to sit on your shoulder?" Harold continued.

"This I've got to see," was heard from the crowd.

Harold put a drop or two of honey on the shoulder of his shirt and then put a jacket on. "Stand near the hive," he instructed. "Then ask your friends if they think you can call the bees to sit on your shoulder. Take your jacket off and whistle. The worker bees will come to your shoulder for the honey spot."

Everyone laughed.

"One last thing," Harold said, "Make sure you give each neighbor a pound of honey from your bees as sweet honey will prevent many complaints."

At one introductory class, Barbara Hoyt, the instructor, noticed a high level of nervousness. This first class of new potential beekeepers asked a barrage of questions about why she kept bees.

"For honey? for beeswax? For pollination?"

"Yes, yes, and yes." She replied. It became apparent that friends and work associates had challenged these new beekeepers on their sanity to keep stinging insects as a hobby.

So, after another barrage of questions during the next class, Barbara informed the class that she keeps honeybees for their wool. Silent, unbelieving stares filled the hall.

"We shear our bees in the spring; being a knitter, I produce bees' wool items during the year." She pulled a yellow knitted glove out of her back pocket, saying, "This is what I knit from last year's shearing, and I expect to get enough wool this year to knit the other glove."

Dead silence, followed by hilarious loud laughter, filled the air. However, the result was that these new beekeepers had a good answer to the "Are you crazy" questions they faced from friends and coworkers.

From then on, The Lost Towns Beekeepers became known as Bees' Wool Beekeepers, with every beekeeper carrying a single yellow mitten in their pocket, ready to be drawn out to answer the question, "Why do you keep bees?"

What began years earlier as a terrible disbanding of towns and uprooting of families became, through laughter and companionship, a gathering and replanting of the wandering roots with The Lost Towns Beekeepers Club.

AUTHOR'S RIDGE
Fred Gerhard

The cemetery in late morning
remains in greening light
warming plush moss — aromatic

On the ridge, two writers listen
sinking into the spongy green
beneath and between

They sit awhile silent
moved by writers here no more
Alcott, Thoreau, others

Gone far below
where roots go
gentle and hard

Ink begins to flow,
first slow, then
rolls out in dappled light

Pressing from elsewhere
transcendent
as moss

These words
these too

HIDDEN BY ROOTS
Heidi Larsen

"Come here my boy."
My grandfather pulled me close
And motioned for me to sit upon his knee.
I was 10 and he was old
As grandfathers tend to be.

I climbed up, and caught a whiff of him:
Ginger for digestion,
Camphor for his old joints,
Add licorice for fun,
Because sweets have their points;
They make up for the
Declining years.

"This is for you."
He held out his pocket watch.
The one he'd carried for as long as I knew.
It's an old silver keepsake
That always kept his time true.

I took it and watched him flip it up.
A foreign engravement,
Signed with an unknown name,
Someone's lost treasure,
That he had somehow claimed.
His brown somber eyes
Now filled with tears.

"I found it buried
Under the root of a tree.
In a small tin box,
recovered first by me,
As an American soldier.

I had enlisted to free
A World at War from its tyranny.
And I stood with the spoils
of war in my hand,
Feeling like a rude excavator,
Knowing someone had hidden it
safe, for later.

The shame of it
I have felt over the years
Numbing my sorrows with some beer."
Then he uttered, "It is yours now."
While staring at me.

"This timepiece is meant to set you free.
I kept it to remind
me to always be kind,
And stand for injustice,
Not act suddenly blind.
So, remember boy,
make your time here count."

MEMORIES OF NEW SALEM ACADEMY
J. A. McIntosh

Marilyn Perry McIntosh graduated from New Salem Academy seventy-seven years ago, on Friday, June 20, 1947. On the following Monday, she went to work for New England Telephone, later Nynex, and presently Verizon. Marilyn married and raised a family in the area. I am the oldest of her two daughters.

Recently, in her Athol home, we sat down to talk about her days at New Salem Academy. Her face still retains the rounded cheeks of her graduation picture, but her hair is gray and she moves slowly. She produced a well-thumbed copy of the 1947 yearbook, *Memories*. She believes that all her classmates are dead, making her one of the oldest surviving graduates of the Academy. Nine people were in her graduating class; she was voted both "best all-round girl" and "best natured girl." Gus Johnson, who went on to run Johnson's Farm in Orange, was "best all-round boy" and Ted Lewis, a long-time resident of Wendell, was "best natured boy."

The yearbook also lists Joseph Ciechon as the principal from 1943 through 1947, but Marilyn clarified that he was drafted in 1944 and returned shortly before graduation. In his absence, Lillian Gardner, a teacher in the commercial program, was acting principal. Mrs. Gardner took a special interest in Marilyn and encouraged her to join the girls' basketball team, even providing her a ride to the games. Marilyn was the team captain in her senior year; unfortunately, they lost most of their games.

Marilyn started her education in a one-room schoolhouse in Moore's Corner, a village north of Leverett. She left the tiny school to go to Amherst High School; the shock of a large college town was not to her liking. In her sophomore year, she transferred to New Salem Academy, where her friend, Viola Williams, was attending. This also solved the problem of transportation, as Viola and her Williams/Carey cousins all made the twelve-mile trip by car to school each day. Dick Carey, a senior at the time, drove, and because Marilyn got picked up last and was the only non-relative, she always ended up sitting in the back, in the middle. They had to push the car up Jennison Road in Wendell when they ran out of gas; once they got to Lake Wyola, they coasted downhill to the gas station in Moore's Corner. During the summer between her sophomore and junior years, Marilyn and her family moved to Orange. She took the bus from Orange to the Academy.

Radios were the primary means of communication and news, and Marilyn's family could not afford to have one in their home. When asked about significant events of her childhood, such as the bombing of Pearl Harbor, VE (Victory in Europe) Day, and VJ (Victory in Japan) Day, Marilyn said she was unaware of the events until she got to school and talked to her friends about the events. Even New Salem Academy did not have a radio. The Class of 1947 class gift was a donation toward purchasing one for the school.

New Salem Academy had customary school subjects, such as math, English, and social studies in the morning. After lunch, each student attended "track" classes. All the boys in the class were on the agriculture track. Marilyn started on the commercial track because her best friend, Viola Williams, was in those classes. She still talks about the difficulties of the math.

In her junior year, Marilyn changed to the home economics track. She got into an argument with the home economics teacher, Mrs. Eaton, for some reason lost to history. Mrs. Eaton told her she had to separate the egg yolks from the egg whites in two dozen eggs for use in the school cafeteria. Marilyn scrambled all the eggs. She declined to say her punishment, but said she never crossed Mrs. Eaton again.

The Class of 1947 was the first at New Salem Academy to take a class trip. They visited Washington, D.C. for April vacation to tour the nation's capital. As far as Marilyn can remember, all the students went. According to the yearbook, the National Library and the Capital were highlights of the trip.

Once a month, assemblies were held in the upstairs hall at the gray, stone Academy building. Everyone in the school, students and staff, would attend. The assembly always started with the Pledge of Allegiance and the New Salem Academy school song. The roots of Marilyn's time at New Salem Academy still run deep. Some seventy-seven years later, she remembers the tune and can sing a few bars of, "Memories, memories, dreams of NSA."

THE ROOTS OF TIME
Aurynanya

Delicate pink petals prance in the breeze,
Branches shake and shiver, without a care.
I search for you in my dreams, waiting,
but you are still not there.
Your bark, ancient and wise,
telling a million stories to live by.
A lifetime of love and dedication,
all gone with the saddest sigh.
Reminding me that the deep rings of time
are nothing to fret or fear
The way you embraced me,
love will always be near.
We've laid down our own rugged roots,
and seeds that weren't afraid to fly.

Our tree of life, strong and resilient,
gone in the blink of an eye
Years and years have passed,
and now I stand strong and alone.
Your spirit endures and will stay
with me until we meet again.
You loved too hard, and
were lost to time, flesh and bone.
I held your hands through my tears
and heartache, I said goodbye
I will always call you mine, mother and father,
I will always call you home.

ROOTED TO EARTH
Marilynn Carter

From the soul of your trunk
ancient roots peek thru earthly layers
rough, gnarled bark
    surrounds your essence
        slither across forest floor

earthly scents permeate air
dew lingers upon brittle leaves

your treasures
    stir, store, transmit
        energy and vibrations
source of strength and power
nutrients needed
    fortify
        building blocks of life
portal to another time
underworld activates memory
    pathway to who you are
awakening to reality
leading the way home

SECONDHAND GARDEN
Phyllis Cochran

When our son, Mike, moved back home after college, he landscaped our yard—a gift my husband and I readily accepted. Mike labored endlessly in the overgrown grassy area pulling up weeds mixed with grass.

Soon our roadside garden was the talk of the neighborhood. Joggers, walkers, and bicycle riders alike would stop to admire and comment about the variety of flowers. Year after year the garden flourished. When I admired the beauty from my window, I thought of my grandfather working daily in his gardens. *Mike must have inherited this gift,* I'd muse.

One May, just as the growing season was beginning, Mike was transferred to a distant location with a new job. My husband and I were left to tend not only our son's dog but a yard dotted with trees, shrubs, and plants, all calling out for attention.

To understand our predicament, one must realize my husband and I were not gardeners. My husband mowed the lawn and that was about it.

And me? Well, I was an indoor type who hated dirt, bugs, and sweat. I wasn't sure we'd ever be able to make the yard look as crisp and bright as when our son pampered it daily.

The roadside garden was particularly vexing, thanks to its conspicuous location in full view to everyone passing by. Unsure of how to proceed, I first tried to ignore it.

One morning I looked out the window and saw children standing in one of the flower plots as they waited for their school bus. How could I let that happen to all Mike's hard work?

A few days later, some purple crocus blossoms caught my eye. They were obviously being hindered by some straggly leaves. I stooped over and removed the offenders. And that's how my life as a gardener began.

The next morning, I decided to work outdoors for a couple of hours. But I was stymied shortly after I started. Unschooled in basic gardening, I couldn't distinguish a weed from a flower.

While intently studying my predicament, young students waiting for their school bus asked what I was doing. They were interested and offered to transplant some violets to another area of our yard before the bus arrived.

During the following week, a middle-aged couple stopped to admire the tulips. I told them I did not know a weed from a flower. They pointed out which plants were weeds. They also gave me some tips about caring for a few perennials.

During the next few weeks, a steady stream of friendly passersby cheered me on or found a moment to offer more gardening hints. Soon, daisies, roses, ground-cover, and other unknown plants were reaching upward for sunlight, adding beauty to the whole yard.

Time has passed since I took those initial, tentative steps into gardening. People stopped and commented about the roadside garden. One summer, two children looking for work even asked if they could weed it. Would you believe it? I became the one pointing out which plants are the unwanted weeds.

Over the years, two of my good friends helped me with transplanting and weeding. Because of them, the garden blossomed every spring.

Now I've moved to a new home. I sometimes feel a beckoning to drive by the old house to see if the garden still exists. After two years, it appears as though the new owners have continued to care for it.

Without the guidance of many caring people, the "secondhand garden" may not have survived. What started out as a dilemma ended as an inspirational lesson.

Mike's gift of love and inspiration live—passed on by my grandfather.

A previous version was published Apr/May 1998 in *Birds & Blooms*. This is a true story about the roadside garden.

HOME IS IN YOUR HEART
LuAnn Thibodeau

There is a trip that I must take.
Although painful, it's a journey I have to make.
A pilgrimage way up north,
The land from which my Mom came forth.

It's a trip that I have put off since Mom died.
What is so heart wrenching to abide,
Mom won't be making the trip with me,
but she'll be watching from Heaven, you see.

I have lived my whole life in the United States of America,
But I feel that I am as much a part of the great country of Canada.
Once a year, we would take our vacation in July,
To this day, this beautiful memory makes me cry.

Since I'm born at the end of April,
I may have been made in the country with the flag of maple.
After my parents visited Canada in July,
Nine months and two weeks later, I came along, oh my my.

To the town of Mom's birth along the shore of Buctouche Bay,
I'll listen to what the mighty Atlantic has to say.
I hope to receive a message from Mom,
To make my heart finally feel calm.

I'll walk through the cemetery,
connecting with others who make up my hereditary.
I'll stop and talk with my Pepère and Mémère there,
listening for words that remind me how much they care.

Pepère died when my Mom was only three
But of course, he is still a part of me.
Mémère died when I was only four,
Sadly I have no memories of this woman so many did adore.
But I'll feel all the love they have for me,
They live in my heart, where they will always be.

I will channel the times I went there with Mom and Dad,
And hopefully those suppressed memories will make me glad.
I'll also visit those remaining members of my family,
Which I know will make all of us extremely happy.

The house where Mom was born I will visit,
As that's almost like a prerequisite.
The beautiful church my Uncle Raymond helped build.
Still sits high upon a lovely hill.

I'll walk the road where Uncle Louie and Aunt Helen used to live,
And remember the wonderful times and all of the love that they'd
give.
Onto the farm of Uncle Willie and Aunt Amanda, remembering how
They taught me to feed the chickens and milk the cow.

Of course, I'll visit with my cousins who still live there,
We'll reminisce about the wonderful times we did share.
All too soon, it will be time to say adios, and not goodbye.
And I know then we all will cry.

I'm aware that all of us are getting up in age,
I pray this won't be the last visit before we turn the final page.
I'll always have the memories to cherish and hold so dear,
As I remember all of the laughter as well as the tears.

This journey will be enlightening and inspiring for me,
And I hope that it will also set some things free.
As the old saying goes: no matter where you roam,
There's no place like home.

I am blessed at home in two wonderful countries,
Where my roots and family ties run deep inside of me.

A SECOND CHANCE AT FINDING MY ROOTS
Catherine H. Reed

Many years ago I went into the hospital for the simple removal of a benign tumor. I was told I would be in for only a few days. I made arrangements for my sister to stay at my apartment to take care of my children. This caused me a lot of stress because I did not go away and leave my children with anyone. But I had no choice. My children were not upset. They loved their Auntie Olly. Olly didn't have children of her own and loved being an Aunty. But sometimes my sister drank too much. She promised she would not drink while she had the children. "I'll take good care of them," she said. I believed her. I had always told her Lynnel and Bruce were half hers. I knew the children would be happy because my sister was a fun-loving person, always laughing and telling funny stories, and a good cook.

I went through the operation but developed an infection. I went into a coma. I could hear everything that went on in the hospital. When family and close friends came to visit I could not talk to them, but I could hear what they were saying. I don't remember the conversations, but they seemed to think I was in serious condition. I do remember feeling very tired.

During this time in my life, I attended church, but I really did not have what we would call today a real relationship with God. In fact I was into a lot of New Age teaching and did not realize it. I had someone contact the church to ask the pastor to come pray for me. He did, and gave me material to read and promised to continue to pray for my healing.

At one point in my stay, I thought I was dreaming, but I was going through a serious encounter. I saw my casket. The rain was pouring down–a huge downpour, a raging storm. Everything was dark, and I was going through a dark tunnel. I remember becoming frightened, and for some reason I knew I was facing death. I was not just facing death; I was dead. It was strange. At that time I did not know anything about anyone having an experience like I was going through. Since then I have heard of many who have had this experience. I thought about my children. I asked God to let me live to raise my two babies, and I promised I would serve Him. I never got an audible answer.

I don't remember what happened next, but one day I woke up. I was very weak. An aide said, "We thought you died," and she just stared at me. She helped me to the bathroom, and I looked in the mirror and my face was green. Yes, green. I became frightened, and then I realized I had

had a near death experience. All I wanted was a quiet time to think this out. I asked that they stop all outside visitors. My stay was twenty-one days. I don't know how long I was in a coma, but I do know it was most of that time. There are many things I don't remember, and I have not tried to find out. All I know is that I was given a second chance at life, and I would be able to raise my babies, and I was grateful to God.

I had wondered why my sister never visited me in the hospital. When I walked into my apartment, my children ran to meet me and hugged me and would not let me go. Then I saw my sister on crutches. She laughed and said, "I didn't let anyone tell you I fell and broke my ankle because I didn't want you to worry about me with the kids. We all managed fine and had a good time." The kids chimed in, all smiles, and said, "Aunty Olly made popcorn every night, and we helped."

Many times I think back on those days and have tried to figure it all out and put the pieces together. One thing I do know is that there is a reason for the second chance and my life will never be the same. God is still working on me, and I am still a work in progress, but I try to let the life I live speak for me. Do I always get it right? No.

Doing God's work was not the problem. I went into the Lay Ministry and did that for fourteen years and loved it. I felt I was keeping my promise to God. But God was showing me through dreams that my work was to be in the ordained ministry, and that was not what I wanted to do. I really did not feel qualified. It was a gradual journey of several years and going to school for formal training. The day I was ordained and presented with my new clergy robe, I had no doubts that this is what I was meant to do. Looking back on all the years I ran from being a minister or a minister's wife, I am grateful that God overlooked my foolish ways and gave me a second chance for the ministry. Today, I too, can say, like my favorite poet, Maya Angelou, "I wouldn't take nothing for my journey."

ROOTS
Fred Gerherd

I.

Chomping off the end of a carrot, peeled and cool
from the fridge, enjoying its earthy watery flavor,
sweet and bitter,

stepping from the porch,
stretching and scrunching toes into warm grass,
feeling roots and the cool loam below

I had barely stood on the earth
a few decades, a few moments, when my mind
turned to roots, my past, my past's past,

a nostalgia for people I never knew
imagining that had they not died I'd be
a little less lonely, and they'd love me in their way.

II.

One ancestor after a good night's sleep,
dreams already being erased by awareness,
stretches as he leaves the mouth of a cave

breakfasting on a prehistoric carrot or spud,
clear crunch in the otherwise empty air,
sun calm and perfect on his naked clay-like skin

presses his toes into the warm turf relaxed
and for a moment we are connected,
tendril toes feeling the earth that seems to know

with a memory like gravity that
roots are an illusion we press into time,
like capillaries conveying an affection for life.

III.

We brush the dust from soles and toes
with our hands and brush our hands of dirt
together, easily in four absent motions

the papery sounds of palm slow upon palm.
The sun takes its time as if to draw us up
to face an azure morning, arms outstretched,

shining for no one to see
where we stand, where we wander
with our roots, cool and bitter, and sweet as dawn.

GYPSY MOTHER
Steven Micheals

It was said she was born in the back of a caravan on a pile of straw, next to a jar of teeth belonging to a creature resembling that of the Loch Ness monster.

But all that was a lie.

Juliet's mother was not a gypsy in the romantic sense, but the stereotypical one. She wandered quite a bit, never taking root, and claiming to have no roots at all. This infuriated Juliet whose lack of identity meant she had to glom onto nearly all sorts of groups for social acceptance and meaning.

At the age of nine, Juliet joined the Girl Scouts. This was useful in that they had rules, an oath, and a uniform, which made up for the complete lack of structure going on in her home life with her aimless mother. Juliet's mother's name was Charlotte. More like *charlatan* because that's what Juliet's mother was. A con artist. Living multiple lives in multiple places and never owning up to who she was or where she came from.

Juliet had decided at some point that her mother was a parasite. Leeching onto other people and using them for money and a means of getting by, so Charlotte didn't have to work a day in her life. It suited her to be on the move, she said.

"We're gypsies," she explained to Juliet, the day of her last Girl Scout meeting as they rode away in their beat-up Volkswagen, the one property that was a constant in their lives. "The world is large, Juliet. It would be foolish to squander our short existence in any one place."

It *really* infuriated Juliet that her mother thought herself a philosopher. It just meant Charlotte was really good at justifying her behavior against the backdrop of a complex universe, as if having a sense of self was just as easy as saying, "I think therefore I am." What nonsense. Juliet thought all the time—if anything, thinking made things worse. Life was full of infinite possibilities which meant a person could have infinite personalities thrust upon them through a variety of circumstances. Her mother was proof of that as she morphed into whomever and whatever the situation demanded. And the more Juliet thought about that, the more envious of her mother she became.

Her mother could become anyone. She could fake accents, forge documents, and look whatever part other people were searching for. Yes, her mother was very much like those gypsies you read about: wandering entertainers with a mysterious past and enough charm to stop anyone from asking too many questions.

Juliet might have eventually become like her if she didn't have such trouble lying. Watching her mother do it so often had caused her only to want to tell the truth. Unfortunately, Juliet did get good at lying to herself.

When Juliet began high school, she became friends with a group of what could only be described as "Goths." This social group was so good at fueling Juliet's angst and somber mood that she nearly became convinced angst and happiness were the same thing. It also didn't hurt that one of the boys in the group was named Derek and that no matter what Derek did, such as sneeze, cough, or even scratch an elbow, it caused Juliet to feel the intense warmth of adolescent love.

Derek. He was a dreamboat by all teen Goth standards. Dark hair, dark painted fingernails, dark circles under his eyes, and a multi-purpose accessorizing chain for all sorts of Goth occasions. He and Juliet "dated" for a year in that they frequently hung out together, and he put his arm around her approximately eight times. Then at the beginning of sophomore year, Derek joined the track team, let the black run out of his hair, stopped painting his nails and the circles under his eyes, misplaced the multipurpose chain, and started making out with Margot Benoit who was blonde and had much bigger breasts than Juliet.

It was then that Juliet took off in the old beat-up Volkswagen. She got five miles out of town and realized she was acting just like her mother. She also realized she wasn't quite old enough to drive and that the police cruiser behind her would most likely show her what real angst was.

Fortunately, Juliet, remembering her Girl Scout promise, pulled over and prepared to be honest, since that was the only thing she was capable of doing with people other than herself. It also helped that the police officer had a daughter and that Juliet had genuine tears. In fact, he had only pulled her over because the brake light was out. She hadn't been driving erratically and her Gothic style suggested someone much older than she was. Furthermore, Juliet was cooperative and the officer allowed her to call her mother on the phone.

After explaining what had happened, Charlotte just laughed and said: "You can try to deny it, but you're my daughter for sure. You felt the need to run. I raised you that way. Running is good. Didn't realize it sometimes takes more courage to run? I think you see that now."

Juliet wanted to hate her mother at that moment, but couldn't. Charlotte spoke with the air of a fortune teller having seen everything play out in her crystal ball.

"I don't want to be you," wept Juliet into the phone.

"I know, sweetie. I don't want you to be me either. You can be whoever you need to be."

"But you always said *we* were gypsies," breathed Juliet. "There's like a wandering in my soul."

Good grief! She heard herself spout near philosophy. There was no escaping becoming her mother now; the tarot cards were drawn.

"Juliet. I may lie to others, but I don't lie to you. I say things, but I never say much to you because you never ask me questions. You think you do, but what have we ever said to one another?"

Juliet thought hard about this. It was true. Her mother and she never talked. More often than not, Juliet just glared at her. When they left on the night of the last Girl Scout meeting, Charlotte's response wasn't in answer to why they were leaving. Juliet had been demanding they stay.

Juliet suddenly remembered her own words that night: "I don't want to leave my friends! You can't make me. You're a horrible mother. You don't care about me."

She had shouted each of those words at her mother. It was the angstiest she had ever been or could ever be. She hated how her mother would uproot them and leave everything behind, especially the friends she so desperately wanted. Friends who wouldn't lie to her, friends her own age, not some grownup who seemingly acted like a child. But Juliet had never asked why they were always running away because she didn't want to hear the truth. That's what happens when you're good at lying to yourself.

And if she had asked why, she would have heard her mother say: *"We can't stay because I'm afraid. I'm afraid people will get to know the real me. I'm afraid they'll take you away from me. You're all I've got."*

Then on the other end of the phone, in her most honest voice, Charlotte said, "I know I'm not a great mother, but I'm your mother. And you're all I've got. Please come home."

Juliet sniffed and muttered in agreement. She handed the phone back to the officer. Eventually, a tow truck came to take the car home while Juliet was escorted by the police. When they arrived at the house, Charlotte thanked the officer and tow truck driver, placed an arm around Juliet's shoulder, and ushered her inside.

They sat next to each other on the couch. They remained silent for a long while.

"I'm sorry," Charlotte said. "I'm sorry for all the things I've done. I'm not proud. I know what you think of me. I wish I were a serious person, but that's not me. I could pretend to be one, like I do everything else, but wouldn't that be worse? This is the most real I'm going to get, kid. Tomorrow I go back to being crazy. It's my coping mechanism. But for the rest of this day, I'll be real. So talk to me."

Juliet would look back on that night and know that she had finally caught a glimpse of her actual mother—not the gypsy, the parasite, or the actress. That night Charlotte was herself. She answered all of Juliet's questions about who her father was and where Charlotte grew up. Her mother was especially good at weaving stories. It distracted her enough from thinking about Derek and how he dumped her as well as the nagging suspicion that he never loved her at all. In the end, it didn't matter whether Charlotte told her the truth or some lies. It only mattered that Charlotte spoke because hearing her mother's voice, even in the back of her mind, meant Juliet would never be alone.

A QUESTION OF COLOR
Clare Kirkwood

In his sonorous Island accent
He said:
"I believe we are all One."
And Yes! He embodies that truth.
And Yes! I believe that truth.
And yet, why the persistent pondering?
Why does the Latina lawyer lament her "whiteness"?
Why do teenagers argue over who looks "lighter"?
Why the surprise when a person who looks "white."
Is seen entering a "black church"?
Why did the woman shudder at the cotton branches
In a lovely floral arrangement?
Was the sharp sting of her ancestor's slavery
Still clinging to her emancipated bones?
Such sinful shame
Of the "paper bag club."
Enter only if you are
"Lighter than a paper bag."
Such travesty in our
"Great Nation's" Capital
Throughout segregation and Jim Crow Laws.
Why at Juneteenth do we chant
"No more chains" in victory?
My tears bleed
Stained with the horror
at the merciless shackles

Our people have endured.
Why the slow dawning of "white privilege"
In the suburb of our awareness?
Why the surprise of African blood
In our "whiteness"?
Why don't we remember
Humanity bloomed in Africa?
Why was the universal
yellow happy face
not enough
To express the panorama
Of emotion
We all encounter?
Why the shades of color in the emojis
When all our blood runs red?
Why is color so important?
Seems we celebrate,
Though late,
the myriad colors
Of band-aids, cosmetics
And "Flesh colored" crayons;
Yet aren't we all searching
For identity and purpose
On our path "To Become One"?

DEAREST BROTHER KAZIMIR
Sharon Ann Harmon

This is a poem written from a true letter sent to my grandfather
Charles (Kazimir) from his brother Jonas in Lithuania.

Grandfather, I read your letter
From your brother Jonas
Postmarked Lithuania 1957

Oceans of distance
Between the pain
Of his love
Trying to make its way
To you across the waves
The deepness of cold
Sweeping to your border
Grief pounding the shore

Brotherly love grounded
In every line he penned
He wrote of illness
He wrote of his son going away to war
He wrote to you about the death
Of your dear son Johnnie
Although the war had swallowed
Johnnie in 1944

In Lithuania, news did not travel fast
I can picture you, drowning in emotion
your hands trembling
Holding that treasured letter

MY ROOTS, MY STRENGTH
Barbara Vosburgh

People often ask why I seem to be so strong. My body isn't that strong, but my desire to push through anything life throws my way is where I hold my strength.

You may be asked where are your roots or where do you come from. What do you say? I come from strength. Born in Dalton, Massachusetts I have carried courage and strength through eight states and the Marshall Islands with many tests along the way.

Where are my roots? I believe they are from the Ukraine and Poland. My paternal grandparents were from the Ukraine and my maternal grandparents were from Poland. Just look at the news if you want to see strength and conviction.

I learned a lot from my grammas. My grandfathers had died before my birth. From my Ukrainian grandmother, I learned hard work is good from growing a garden to milking her one cow. I saw my first chicken beheaded and served for dinner. While other grandmothers were baking cookies and going to the park with their granddaughters, my grandmother was teaching me the proper way to iron a shirt, sweep a floor, and make a bed. She taught me to take pride in any kind of work I did no matter if I liked it or not. I also learned to always expect a sweet treat when she came to visit.

Gramma B also showed me that when life throws you lemons laced with vinegar, you pick them up, wash them off, and take one step forward at a time and cook a chicken. I was told my grandfather died suddenly. Gramma could barely speak English, and she had children at home. She didn't give up or give in. Gram grew her own food in the garden and raised chickens plus she got milk from her cow. She then went to work in the paper mill plus cleaned other people's houses. A boarder rented out a room in her duplex house in a section of town called Cotton Town, and I remember the white picket fence in the front yard and all the beautiful flowers she grew. Gramma B raised seven children, putting five of them through college. My dad was old enough to quit school and work to help put his siblings through school.

When two of my uncles lost their wives, it was Gramma B who went to cook, clean, and take care of the children. I rarely saw her without an apron on and a pot on the stove. She smiled a lot, but when she was upset with me, I knew.

My Gramma B was a strong, brave lady who met life head on no matter what. She passed away when I moved to Alabama. If someone had contacted me when I was still in Maryland, I would have been there for her.

Then there was my Polish gramma. I was told my Polish grandparents were quite wealthy in Poland but left the country with nothing. Not knowing the date of their departure, I can only speculate. When they arrived at Ellis Island, they made their way to Pittsfield, Massachusetts. Grandpa worked, but I was told he gave very little money to my grandmother to feed and clothe the four children at home. He spent most of his money on his friends at the local pub. My mom repeatedly told me about the coat her father bought her, and she said nothing else about my grandfather.

Gramma K had a wonderful sense of humor. I did not speak Polish. She did not speak English, but somehow we understood each other. She tried to teach me Polish songs and to count. I wasn't very good. When my mom was passing, I sang her one of Gramma's songs in Polish. It calmed her down. I remember Gramma K coming to live with us briefly before she had to go to a nursing home. I was so sad and did not understand until later in life that she had Alzheimers. Years later my stepdad had it, and I was blessed to be able to work with Alzheimer patients doing activities. Gram passed when I was 15. I had to take the bus trying to be with her, but it was too late.

Then there were my parents, first generation Americans. My dad was the hugger and the fun one while my mother was the disciplinarian without a sense of humor. Dad worked in a paper mill as a beater engineer, and Mom was a stay at home housewife. Dad took me ice skating, fishing, and swimming, and made hot chocolate for all my friends. Mom told me to keep my room clean and not get into any trouble.

Dad became very ill with cancer, but still mowed my Uncle Bill's lawn for him. Bill had polio. When I was ten, Dad passed away. I remember the lines of people at the funeral home. He was well loved.

Mom sat down in the kitchen the day after the funeral and cried all day. She had my brother who was preparing to go to college the following fall, and me to take care of all alone. Mom had not finished high school because, like my dad, she was expected to quit school and work to help the family. Did that stop her? No way. She enrolled in a business school, got straight A's in all her classes, found a good job, and put my brother through college. Strength! Mom asked me once why I did so much myself instead of calling a handyman. I just said, "Mom, where do you think I get all my strength?" I watched my mom go through so much for years, and she came out the other side just as strong and determined as ever.

I am not going to talk about all the times I needed and still need to be strong. Much of it I do not even share with friends or family. Just know I have surprised people, including doctors, with my strength and determination. Where do I get it from? My Ukrainian and Polish roots of course. I have brought those roots with me everywhere I wandered throughout my life, and I hold them dear to my heart. Bring your own roots and story with you held next to your heart as you travel life's journey. They will not let you down.

Bare Roots

SOCKS: A LOVE STORY
Diane Hinckley

Socks mate for life. When you purchase ten pairs of foreign-made socks in a plastic bag and mix them up in the laundry, you are breaking up couples and causing dramas worthy of a TV reality show. One devoted sock couple, Francesca and Paolo, found themselves condemned to quick glimpses of one another flying around in the dryer.

By contrast, from the day Wanda Parmenter carried them home from the Christmas craft fair, the alpaca socks that called themselves Winston and Marilyn faced no threat to their love beyond jealous remarks in the sock drawer and male socks' occasional efforts to seduce the soft and shapely Marilyn. A persistent argyll sock named Lachlan was fond of telling Marilyn "What happens in the bureau stays in the bureau." But even Lachlan's sexy Scottish accent, knowing manner, and heathery broodiness failed to lure Marilyn's attention from her beloved Winston—at least not to the point of doing anything she shouldn't.

Marilyn and Winston were children of the Central Massachusetts earth, dyed with colors wrung from wild mushrooms and the lichen that drapes the rocks of the ancient stone walls of New England. Local craftswoman Bliss MacKenzie made Winston from the wool of her pet male alpaca, Pyramus. She fashioned Marilyn from the lush fleece of her female alpaca, Thisbe. And both of those useful beasts subsisted on hay acquired from the farm of Gerald "Grease" Willoughby, local autodidact and self-described Constitutional scholar. "All flesh," the Bible tells us, "is grass," and, via Pyramus and Thisbe, Winston and Marilyn's flesh was the grass of Central Massachusetts, down to its tangled roots. Winston and Marilyn understood this land, and they understood and adored each other.

Although the socks couldn't see each other when Wanda's boots were laced up for a hike at the Quabbin or on Northfield Mountain, each felt comfort in the other's presence and in the shared task of trudging over glacial erratics and gnarled roots. Later, while enjoying a thorough but gentle hand washing, they murmured their impressions of the day to one another. They would then enjoy spending the whole night on the drying rack, dripping into the bathtub, away from the strained dynamics of the sock drawer.

Once a year, Wanda took a trip to some exotic land. At Machu Picchu, Winston and Marilyn felt the heaviness in Wanda's step as she fought the altitude. One evening, in a pub on Ireland's Dingle Peninsula, Wanda fell over a chair while attempting an inebriated jig. One of her boots flew off, striking the piper in the knee. Winston, left naked on Wanda's foot, got a good look at the ensuing scuffle and the laughing faces. He saved it all for the entertainment of Marilyn, as they later lay on Wanda's hotel room floor.

In rugged Patagonia, Winston and Marilyn found themselves on the floor of a hotel room that was not Wanda's. Winston could see under the bed and right to the other side, where another, larger pair of alpaca socks smirked back at him. They were younger and fluffier than Winston and Marilyn, with no darning or fraying. Winston pondered the passage of time and the wear and tear on socks. To Winston, Marilyn had grown only more beautiful with time.

Dawn saw Wanda leaping out of bed and donning her jeans and sweater in a flurry, while some laughing fellow kept trying to pull her in for a kiss. She giggled, grabbed her shoes and socks, and fled over the threshold, dropping Marilyn on the way. Back in her own room, she threw her clothes willy-nilly into a duffle bag before running down the stairs to a waiting bus.

Lying among the jumbled clothes in the duffle bag, first in the bus and then on the flights home, Winston tried to convince himself that Marilyn was elsewhere in the bag, safe under a pair of underpants or wrapped around a fragile souvenir. She couldn't be gone. She couldn't be left behind.

"Oh, drat!" said Wanda, turning her duffle bag upside down on the living room rug. "That was my favorite pair of socks."

"For crying out loud," said her twin sister, Wendy. "You were just in South America. You could have bought a new pair of alpaca socks. Or vicuna, or whatever they have in Argentina."

"I loved those old socks. I've been everywhere in those socks. I met Juan in those socks."

"Juan," scoffed Wendy. "Have you heard from Juan?"

"I just got back!" Wanda wished she hadn't told Wendy about the handsome Argentine, Juan. She knew her sister thought she was a chump who mistook a vacation fling for a romance. Oh well, maybe she was a chump, a romantic chump.

"Has he texted?" persisted Wendy.

Wanda clutched her beloved, now unmated, sock for comfort. She supposed she could use it as a dust rag.

"That would make a great sock puppet for little Dwight David," said Wendy.

Yeah, Wanda supposed. She could turn the sock into a puppet for Wendy's kid to abuse until it fell apart.

Days went by with no word from Juan. Wanda left the lone alpaca sock draped over the copy of Dante's *Inferno* she'd been bogged down in since before her trip, until one evening, tired of brooding over lost love, she got out her sewing basket and box of stray buttons and began searching for a matching pair of buttons for the puppet's eyes. She was starting to think she would have to settle for one button eye and a raffish eye patch, when the doorbell rang.

Startled, she turned on the outside light and peered out a window. She clutched her cell phone in case she needed to call 911 about a weirdo on her doorstep. And there was Juan, with a suitcase in his left hand. His right hand was in his jacket pocket.

Wanda threw open the door. Juan brought a cloth object from his pocket. "You forgot your sock," he said.

A LIFE LESSON FROM THE OLD CELLAR DOOR

Elaine Daisy McKay

The house that we live in is very old
Parts have been remodeled, but not so the old cellar door.
It hangs rather funny though it has had much repair
But it carries a jewel to which none can compare.

For the back of this door is our family delight.
It has captured life, with children's eyes so bright.

The grandchildren's growth, the age and the year,
Have been marked and written by Papa so dear.
'Tis a glorious event each Thanksgiving Day
As each child stands for his mark so clear.

Their faces glow when they stretch themselves tall
For that mark will tell all, forever in time.
They step back and turn, with their eyes so proud,
To see how they have grown, in one year gone round.

There was quite a fuss, a few years ago
When I felt the old cellar door just had to go.

I'd redone the kitchen, with paper & paint
So as I opened the door and peered at those marks,
I paused and I said, I can transfer those lines
To a brand new door and it will even hang straight.

But Papa said, "Whoa, for goodness sake.
No question about it, a vote this will take."

Needless to say, as I look at it now, I stood alone in my futile attempt.
It was with eyes I had voted and not with my heart.
The children and Papa were firm on that day,
A treasure they had, they weren't changing,
no way.

So, Lestoil and I, we visited that door.
I really must say, I hadn't tried that approach
With such vigor before.
Not a mark was erased, the names kept their place
Changed the water three times, for that was the case.

Now the door sparkles and a bit with pride.
If doors could talk, she'd surely voice her side.

"Ha ha ha. Ha. I'm more than a door,
I'm a keeper of time, such as you have never seen before
I've held this family as life moved along
I've carried this record like the tune of a song."

I believe each one of us if we thought of it now
Would realize how doors play such a part of our lives.
Some we can see like the old cellar door.
Some are opportunities in the walkway of life.

Some we will open, some we best shut, and not walk through.
Nevertheless, a door placed before us, ever so true.

The decisions of doors must come right from the heart,
To simplify us all right from the start.

In my grandchildren's lives, they will have many doors.
But perhaps the old cellar door, on its crooked old hinge
Will carry a lesson on memory's wings.

Because the grandchildren, yes, you and I indeed
With wisdom and love, we too,
must continue to meet life's many doors.

WE WILL NEVER KNOW
Cathy Carlton Hews

There's a reason I don't, I haven't, written about her. Many, actually, very many. Friends have remarked on her absence from my first book, *A Bagful of Kittens Headed for the Lake*. She was adopted as an infant and developed serious mental health, abandonment issues, along with decades of substance abuse. Yeah, I would say there's a reason, many reasons, for that. Fuck off.

I pushed her out of my mind for decades. If I don't think about her, I have a life. When I do think about her, I don't. Not thinking about her, I'm all grown up and can go shopping, work, read a book, pull my panties on, do the dishes, and play with these stupid cats. I can do those things instead of cowering in a corner.

All grown up now, I can flee from one side of the country to the other. Often. I can divorce after being married for forty-five minutes. I can have unhealthy relationships with men. I can cut friends out of my life if I feel aggrieved. *Don't cross me, motherfuckers.* I can move from apartment to apartment, never settle down, never be "home" somewhere.

I'm all grown up now. I get to do all those things.

I have, however, been aware of the swirly hole of sorrow somewhere in the middle of me. Swirly, like sparkly, gray, flowing chiffon. Recently, sorrow was always in motion, feeling like the wind. Sometimes, the better times, the chiffon fluttered softly, like a spring breeze. Those times, the better times, I was able to walk around with it, barely noticing the hole. Other times, the bad times, the chiffon blew sharply as if it were tormenting Auntie Em's clothesline during a Kansas tornado. Those times, I could barely walk around, pain piercing the middle of me. I recognize that pain from when I was a girl, living under the same roof as my mother.

I was born in Presque Isle, Maine, about as far north as you can get in the U.S. My parents, my brother and I, and Rex, the family dog, lived in a remote township called Ashland. The land area was called The Ridge. There was no official address. Mail came to a rural route number.

The Maine years were probably the best she could ever be, before the rage took her.

She was funny and bright. She wore bright pink pedal pushers. She was ambitious, and she wanted better for me. Later I realized she wanted better for *herself.* She wanted to be a writer, she was jealous as I started to publish my own work.

I'm smart and funny and quick. I got that from her. However, I was a teenager when I began to recognize the swirly hole in her. Of course, not knowing what it was, I watched it blow. Sorrow and anger formed an unrelenting gale inside her. My father and brother kept their heads down and held on to whatever they could clutch.

I began to separate, emotionally, but especially physically, from them at an early age. I thrived in school, I planned never to be home. I lived my life outside of their house. The wind was not going to take me.

Years later, during one of my stays in Los Angeles, I forget which, one of the times I moved there and then moved back east and then moved back to L.A., I began to identify my own swirly hole. Ahhh, it's her, I have no family, no background. OK.

This knowledge gradually creeps up on you. *When did you realize your mommy wasn't like all the other mommies?* Much easier to pretend you don't have a mommy. Or an enabling daddy or brother, for that matter.

Not too much later, suddenly, I was back east again for (maybe) the last time.

Yay, I get to move back east again and take care of Dad with Alzheimer's, because everybody else is dead. After a few years, he was dead, too.

I plodded on, back in the small town. I forgot to leave the small town and settled in (somewhat). I had a job at a college I loved, with a community I loved, friends I loved. Well, as much as I could love anything, which wasn't much. Plus I had the two stupid cats.

I began to take classes at the college. One of the classes I stumbled into dealt with memory. Memory and attachment theories. My ears pricked up during these studies. The science of attachment drew me in and I began to write about my past in class.

My mother was adopted, and I began to wonder about that. What happened in those circumstances that could have turned a little baby into ... her?

I was excited and relieved. Oh, hey, here's something to blame! Science, let's blame science? Something happened to her as soon as she slid out of the womb, and that explains it all! Whew, what a relief. It's NOT that she never loved anything, right?

Hey, Mommy, can you bake cookies for my third-grade class tomorrow can you buy me a new dress can you cook and make us dinner I would love a casserole hey Mommy can my friends come over hey Mommy can we put up a Christmas tree this year so the other kids won't think we are weird freaks who don't have a tree...

She would look at me, not say a word, and bark at my hapless little brother to make her another drink.

Science will explain it! As the class continued and I learned more and more about memory and the brain, I zeroed in on early attachment theories. Basically, if you didn't have this or that going on as soon as you toddled your little self through kindergarten and probably first grade, you were fucked.

Well, there you go, I thought, all grown up and college-y. That explains it.

She talked about her adoption a lot. It certainly was imprinted on her. I remembered her saying she was from The Home for Little Wanderers.

I began to dig. For the first time in my life I was getting curious about her beginnings. What had happened to her, early on? How did she start out in life?

She would say, "I'm from the Home for Little Wanderers" often, as if to remind us that, yes, adoption, awful. Yeah, yeah, yeah, we get it. I protected myself by engaging with her as little as possible, and I always brushed off her self-pity.

But now I was interested because I had learned about attachment theories. The Home was a valuable starting place. I searched, and lo and behold, it popped up right away. That surprised me, as my mother was born in the mid-'30s, I think.

What's still standing from the mid-'30s? The Home looked like a big operation now, with several branches, some in Maine. I thought she started life in Maine, so I called the most likely branch, in Waterville.

Rosie, a cheery receptionist answered and chirped, "Hi, Home for Little Wanderers! How may I help you?" Only I don't think she said that; I think she chirped, "Hi, Maine Children's Home." Hmm, name change, well, OK. She and I stumbled through *hi my name is Cathy Hews and I am looking for information about my mother, Shirley Hews, born in the 1930s she was adopted through you guys to a family in northern Maine and apparently all didn't go well as she was a miserable bitch all her life and hated everything around her—her own family included—this especially fucked me up and it somewhat fucked up my brother and father they were lucky cause they didn't know HOW fucked up they were ahh I wish I didn't know how fucked up I was but I did Rosie I did I always knew how fucked up I was she was always batshit crazy hahahaaa Rosie what's that old Maine saying my father used to call her oh yeah crazier than a cat shot in the ass hahahaah well she was Rosie I'm all grown up now I'm sixty-six right that's a long time to be fucked up whooo daddy but there you have it and get this Rosie I'm in college now right hahahahaha hey its a start maybe I will make something of myself after all anyway Rosie I started taking this class about memory and one section was about attachments and how babies and little kids were fucked from the jump if there wasn't a healthy attachment I know GET ME talking all smarty pondering healthy attachments hahahaaha those college kids are really smart though wow I'm struggling to keep up well anyway I got to thinking maybe just maybe she was a horrible nasty blood-sucking bitch because something or other didn't form when it was supposed to I'm not excusing her no way Rosie but everybody avoided her and I got the fuck out*
when I was eighteen fuck her right Rosie anyway I got to wondering about what happened to this miserable bitch when she crawled out of hell and slid her cloven hooves into those ratty slippers so that's why I'm calling.

Pause.

"One moment please," Rosie.

Rosie is back after a while and says whomever I need to speak to isn't in right now and why don't I leave my number and someone will get back to me?

OK, I say, somewhat hesitantly. *But you get me Rosie right I really would like to know a little more about Mommy's deal what can you tell me?*

Rosie, carefully, says "Well, we would have to look into it, you see. I will pass this along. What was your mother's date of birth again? Thank you, and what number is best to reach you? Thank you. We will try to locate her records —a long time ago, though—and I will call you back as soon as I have some information.

OK, I say. *Don't forget me, Rosie,* I thought.

Rosie called me back a couple of weeks later.

"Well, good news and bad news," she says.

What?

"We indeed found your mother's records."

Great!

"But they're sealed."

What? Really? It's only me left. All the players here are dead.

"I'm so sorry, but the state law maintains confidentiality even after death."

Well, that doesn't make a lot of sense to me, Rosie. Honestly.

She hemmed and hawed, a tad sympathetically.

"I would recommend calling your state legislators, also the Maine ones. You are not the only person coming to us looking for records."

"Yeah, yeah," I said. "I'll be sure to do that."

Truth be told, I didn't really give a fuck about my mother's specific circumstances.

Why should I? She didn't ever give a fuck about my specific circumstances, the suffering she inflicted. Anyway, that's what I told myself as I stamped my mental foot on the mental floor. I was an all grown-up sixty-six abandoned baby, too, and I was still furious, heartbroken.

I convinced myself I was more interested in the general circumstances of babies being dumped off. What happens, like in the science-y way? Surely there is an explanation of why she was her. I just needed to know that.

OK, Rosie, well, what can you tell me? Is there anyone there who can fill me in on the generalities of adoptions, maybe an admin person and/or a psych person? I can connect the dots for myself, I guess.

Rosie shifted uncomfortably, I guessed. I pictured her as young, hair in a ponytail with a blue ribbon, a shift dress, pink with yellow daisies, blue eyeshadow to match the ribbon, her shoes Mary Jane knock-offs, and Rosie smelling vaguely of the chicken salad she made this morning for lunch.

I assumed she was shifting in her chair due to the following awkward pause or she was getting hungry for lunch, or both. She finally said, "Oh yes, there are people here who can speak with you. I will ask the assistant director to contact you. Would you like to set up a Zoom appointment?"

Oh, no, I said, I'm coming up to the area in person. I would like to speak with someone directly.

"Oh, OK," she said. "I will look at his schedule and make an in-person appointment. Oh, and there is a small administrative fee, you know, for processing, and record-finding."

Huh?

"Oh, a small fee."

So, because I want to understand, I'm traveling from another state to get up there to talk to some folks who can't even give me any specific information about my mother, and I'm paying for the privilege?

Stammering—and here I picture her twirling the blue ribbon out of her hair—"Yes, I'm sorry. It's a small administrative fee…"

How much?

"$75.00."

Now I am the one pausing. Finally, I say, OK, Rosie, if you could set that appointment up for me that would be great. Thanks for your help.

It was the morning of the Maine trip and I was already late before I left the apartment. Kitty litter stinkin', dishes piled up, suitcase unpacked; I was dragging my heels on getting this party on the road. Rosie had offered a Zoom option; wouldn't that be smarter? No, I had said, aforementioned heels dug in. I was determined to make the trip as… what? The last pilgrimage to the land of my birth? Some pseudo-romanticized Miss Marple-y mission to unravel the mysteries of my mother? Please. Some bullshit like that?

There were to be two stops in Maine, and the first was Waterville, the orphanage town. Waterville was a four-hour drive, so I settled in. The appointment was the next morning, and I wanted to get there before dark, though the late start didn't help me.

"Oh hey, you're going to Maine! Wow, how beautiful. Lucky you! It's gorgeous there this time of year. Go up the coast and stop in those little towns by the ocean. Have lots of lobsters and clams rolls and then have more lobsters. You're SO lucky."

Friends have been squealing some version of this for weeks now. I would snort every time.

"Uhhh, I'm not from the pretty part of Maine, my darlings. I'm from the North. No lobsters, no clam rolls, no ocean. But there ARE potatoes and woods. Lots and lots of woods."

"Oh," they would say. "Well can't you make a quick detour to Pretty Maine?"

"No, one place in Maine is at least four hours from the other place. So no."

"Oh."

I wanted to go to Pretty Maine. I wanted the lobster and clam roll and the Atlantic.

But no. In my years growing up there, I never saw Pretty Maine. I saw sawmills and potatoes, though. My grandfather worked for a sawmill and my dad would take my brother and me over to the mill where we would slide down these enormous piles of sawdust, higher than a house. While not lobster or a clam roll, it was fun for a little kid.

Many years later, I was living in New York City and the first time I saw Pretty Maine was on my honeymoon.

After slogging through Massachusetts and New Hampshire, I approached the Kittery Bridge, the portal to Maine. I remember it well, though it must have been forty years since I crossed it. My dad always mentioned it as we approached it. "Hey, look now, here's the Kittery Bridge." I could hear his voice as I approached it.

A couple of hours later, close to Waterville now, I stopped at another rest stop for gas. You know you're in Maine when there's a large moose statue standing proudly outside the parking lot. Before I left, there had been a dispute among friends about moose. A few had the temerity to question the existence of the Maine moose.

"C'mon, Cathy, Maine keeps insisting on the existence of their prized moose population, but no one ever sees one. *Daddy do you see a moose no dear I don't see no moose.* I rose up on my Maine haunches, whiskers pricking, nostrils flaring, and retorted, "There most certainly ARE moose in Maine, how dare you? I'll take a picture of one on the trip for you!"

"You do that, Cathy."

Smart asses. I took a picture of the rest stop moose. A friend texted me, "Oh I know where you are. There's a statue of a bear at the plaza on the other side."

Soon after that I landed at the motel. Well, I'm here. "OK, Shirley, let's finally go see what's what."

The next morning, I pulled into the driveway. It was a beautiful, sunny day. I watched a bunch of little kids playing on the playground right in front of me. There were four or five caretakers. Good, I noticed to myself, the ratio of adults to kids was OK. That worry was checked off my list. There were a couple of Black kids. Good, I noticed to myself, probably racially diverse. Some little girls were playing on the seesaw, whereas on the other side of the playground, boys were tearing up dirt and jumping off an old stump—it was all very *Cider House Rules* with its *Goodnight you, Princes of Maine.*

I had pictured The Home for Little Wanderers as rather Dickensian—gruel; harsh, inattentive matrons; lights out at seven o'clock; maybe a half hour outside for recess; hand-me-down rags; the switch if you were bad. But everybody looked happy and well-fed. Hmm, not the gruel diet. Well, I suppose that changed over the last century. I kept looking at the babies being rocked by their caregivers. That would have been nice. I hope Mom had that.

I sat in the car a good while and watched the kids, choking back … well I don't know what I was choking back … something. *Did you ever have that, Cathy? Did someone rock you like that? I don't know, stop asking me. I remember one fun thing as a little kid: my first birthday. Yes, I do remember that I was sitting in a high chair at Grammie's, facing out in the yard. There was cake, and I wore a little red and white striped baby suit and everybody was laughing.*

Choking back the something, I got out of the car and entered The Home for Little Wanderers.

A nice receptionist met me. "Welcome to the Maine Children's Home. The program director, Matt, will be right with you."

Matt was a young, thoughtful-looking counselor, and he guided me to an outside picnic table. We could still see the kids playing.

Awwwww, when do they go in and get their gruel? Do they then take a nap? And then do they get the switch before they go back outside and then come in and have more gruel before they sob themselves to sleep?

"Well," Matt said. "No kids live here. It's a daycare program."

Oh, really? No kids live here? Then how does the orphanage thing work?

Well, we are not an orphanage. We are an adoption agency.

No gruel, no tear-stained pillowcases?

No. There was an orphanage in Boston way back, but not at this location.

So, I'm looking at attachment theories. I hoist myself up, all college girl. And I was thinking there must have been a disconnect in her brain somehow. (WHY WAS SHE HERE? WHY?)

Well, we wouldn't know. She would have been adopted straight out of here.

So, arrangements were made and she went directly to the adoptive parents?

Yes. He shoved a pile of self-help-y books at me. *Trauma and You, Adoptive Parents and the New Baby, When Adoptions Go Awry.*

He talked some more about the agency now. Thirty staff people, sixteen counselors, comprehensive programs for prospective adoptive parents, the many training programs for staff on trauma, LGBTQI+ friendly, non-denominational, grief counseling, planned parenthood, pro-choice. I nodded my head at times, speechless. I could sense he felt a little sorry for me.

So, what I had previously thought were the circumstances of my mother's early years were, uhh, probably not?

He looked at me.

"No," he said.

So, we don't really know?

No. That being said, there are cases of adoption disruption. Sometimes, rarely, an adoption just doesn't work. The families are brought in for extensive counseling.

Do you see many families dealing with dysfunctional adoptions?

Uhh, well...

My voice rose. "Am I the only family member coming in with stories of dysfunctional adoptions?

He looked at me. (There's that sorrowful look again.) "Yes."

He then wanted to introduce me to the Executive Director. I was led upstairs to a room resembling Dumbledore's office. There were old, beautiful, oak furniture pieces and an ornately blue-and-gold-brocade sofa. I sat in a heavy wooden chair.

After a few minutes, she entered. She started speaking to me, soft and low, in that Minerva McGonagall way, wise and firm.

"When they told me you were coming, I asked the staff, 'What does she think I can tell her?' I didn't even look at your mom's file. I didn't want to know the circumstances since I cannot share anything with you."

She went on about the history of the Home, and the future of the Center. She reiterated what Matt had said regarding the staffing, accreditation and training programs.

NO, I WANT TO KNOW EXACTLY WHAT HAPPENED HERE THAT MADE HER...HER.

"Sometimes families just need to talk. I'm here to listen"

NOT HELPFUL, MRS. MCGONAGALL. I NEED TO KNOW. ARE YOU

SORRY FOR ME? IS EVERYBODY HERE SORRY FOR ME AND HUMORING

ME? I HAVE SPENT THREE MONTHS ON RESEARCH FOR THIS QUEST AND I NEED TO KNOW WHAT HAPPENED HERE TO EXPLAIN ... HER.

I didn't exactly put it like that, but I feebly sputtered out something along those lines.

She talked about the history of U.S. adoptions and the orphan trains. Both Maine and Canada separated Indigenous children from their families.

I listened.

Finally, she said to me, quietly, about my mother, "We have to accept that we will never know."

I sat there. I got up. I thanked her. I walked slowly back to the car.

I sat in the car for a while. The kids were all gone from the playground.

I put the car in gear and headed north for the last Maine stop, Presque Isle, where I was born.

481 MILLBURY STREET

Sharon Ann Harmon

I click pictures of Millbury Street,
the boarded windows,
gray asphalt shingles, dying tree.
Your grandparents from Poland
owned that house, my mother had told me.

Let's go in, I say to my daughter, it
will be ripped down soon and gone forever.
She is seventeen and full of adventure.
I am forty-eight and looking for roots.
We climb the back stairs to the second floor,
go into a stench of decay.
Warily walking through rubble.
I want to find something that could have
been theirs,
but what could be left from 1925?

I relate stories I've been handed down,
as nesting pigeons startle us.
"Let's leave," I say, feeling sad,
but seeing an understanding light in my daughter's eyes.

I see wallpaper from
the seventies and then I notice the front hallway,
what appears to be original wallpaper hanging in sheets.
A very old pattern of ferns, leaves, and flowered urns
covering horsehair plaster behind it. Brittle, yellowed,
and musty, I know it is the paper they lived with.

I carefully rip two large pieces.
I have five brothers and my daughter to divide it among.
Some people are left with legacies and wealth,
I feel my grandparents' presence
and lovingly guard my heirloom treasure.

This was previously published in *Worcester Magazine* and Harmon's chapbook *Swimming With Cats*.

SECRETS
Larry Barrieau

When I was in the seventh grade, Pep Casey said that he was going to take me fishing at Lake Winnipesaukee in New Hampshire. This was very exciting news because Winnipesaukee is a huge lake, and I was used to little Laurel Lake in Fitzwilliam. Another exciting thing was that this was to be an overnight excursion. I was packed and ready two weeks before we went.

Pep picked me up in the morning. In the front seat was his friend from work, Mr. Sawyer. I put my stuff in the cargo area of the Rambler station wagon, climbed into the back seat, and waved goodbye to my mum on the porch. With Pep's small boat in tow, we headed for the big lake.

I loved to go places, so my head was swiveling to see everything. In about forty-five minutes, Massachusetts and the last of the familiar sights were in the rearview mirror. The men in the front mostly talked of their workplace, Simplex Time Recorder, and gossiped about bosses and coworkers. I didn't care about that and watched the New Hampshire scenery pass by. This part of New Hampshire was more rural than even Fitzwilliam. Pretty farmhouses and barns dotted the rolling hillsides. Cows near the roads lifted their heads to look at us as we passed and kept right on munching. Going through Manchester, we crossed the big Merrimack River, and Pep said that it emptied into the ocean where he would sometimes fish for cod.

The signs for the lake were getting numerous, and I was straining to catch a glimpse of it. Soon, we were turning into our motel which was on a very small canal that led into the big lake only a few hundred yards away, although I couldn't see it yet. The modest motel with bare essentials had board walls with no paint. "Knotty pine" indicated a decorative decision and not its real purpose—an inexpensive way to build a motel.

After unpacking, we went out for supper. This was another big deal because our family seldom went to a restaurant or even a hot dog stand. On the way back to the motel, we drove by Weirs Beach so I could see the lake. It was like looking at a bay in the ocean, and Pep said that it was only a tiny part of the lake.

"Just wait till we get around that island tomorrow and you'll see," he said in a voice that indicated he was a little excited himself.

When we got back to the motel it was getting dark, so I went out to explore a little. At the end of the pier, where we had tied up the boat, was a gas pump *just* for boats. It had never occurred to me that there was such a thing. At Laurel Lake, we just grabbed a gas can and filled it at the Esso station. A kid not much older than me ran the pump, making change from a roll of dollars in one pocket and coins in another. Under a single light with moths flitting around his head, he seemed much older than he was. He chatted up the boat owners, made small talk about the weather, and even shared fishing tips—where they were, what bait to use, and what pound test the line should be. As I walked back to our room, I turned around to see the kid, animated, gesturing, and laughing. I wished I could be as cool as him, nonchalant, and comfortable in his little oasis of light.

Back in the room, Pep and Mr. Sawyer were getting ready for bed. Pep and I would share the bed and Mr. Sawyer would sleep on the cot. There was the smell of old man crap in the bathroom, so I tried to hold my breath but couldn't. When I got out, I crossed the room and took a deep breath to clean out the smell. In bed, I pulled the covers up and thought about the next day and the big fish I would brag about back home. The men had a final farting contest thinking it was hilarious. I think I had to agree!

The sun hadn't risen as I got dressed, and the men grunted and groaned as they bent over to put their socks on. Pep asked Mr. Sawyer how he had slept. Mr. Sawyer was grumpy and in a thick New Hampshire Yankee accent said, "Son of a bitch, I've slept on softah sument!" Pep chuckled, and I laughed out loud.

There was a diner only a few hundred feet from the motel, so we walked to breakfast as it was getting lighter. A thick, gloomy fog hung low, and I was worried that we might have to cancel the fishing, but Pep looked up and announced that the fog would burn off in an hour. A short time later, we had the boat in the water and were putting up the Weirs Channel and into the big lake. The sun was shining, and I was very impressed with my grandfather's forecasting ability.

Leaving the channel, the expanse of the lake struck me. There were islands in Winnipesaukee that were bigger than Laurel Lake itself. I moved quickly from one side of the boat to the other to get a better view as if the scene was going to disappear before I could take it all in. As we passed close to some islands, an optical illusion occurred. While staring at them, it felt like we were sitting still and they were the ones moving, gliding by as if caught in a lazy current. Pep, having been born there, recited their names in a litany from his childhood. I pictured him at my age, exploring that wondrous place.

Our fishing poles were big and sturdy like ocean poles, and they were baited with spoons and minnows. We trolled all three lines behind us and let out enough line so that the lures would be near the bottom. I had not seen fishing line like that before. It had a lead core to make it sink, and it was a different color every twenty feet or so. The colors would tell you how much line was out and so it also worked as a fathometer.

A couple of lake trout were caught, but only by Pep. He saw that I wasn't doing too well, so when he hooked yet another fish, he gave me the pole and told me to reel it in, he needed a beer. It was heavy, and I had to reel in over a hundred feet of line. When I got the trout close to us, he put the net under it and swung it into the boat. It wasn't a large fish compared to other lake trout, but compared to the little brook trout I was used to catching, it was a monster. My wrists were a little sore, but I was proud that, *together*, we landed a nice one.

At mid-day, we took a break from fishing, and opened up the cooler for lunch. My mother had made me sandwiches and put in snacks and drinks too. The sandwiches were fluffernutters, the snacks were Hydrox cookies, and the drinks were Cokes. The men were provisioned by their wives, and the only thing I remember about their lunch was the pile of Pabst Blue Ribbon beer cans on shards of ice that took up most of the room in the cooler. A white plastic can opener with the words "Brazell's Package Store" printed on it, a translucent red button, and a large "church key" hung lashed to one of the cooler handles.

Late in the afternoon, we headed back in, pulled the boat onto the trailer, and started for home. The early morning wake-up, the sun, and the wind made us all tired, so Mr. Sawyer got in the back to sleep and I sat up front with Pep. We planned to stop in an hour or two for supper. I didn't know what I would have for my meal, but dessert would surely be blueberry pie.

After watching the scenery go by for a while, I nodded off a couple of times. I woke up and was looking at a pretty white-water river that flowed near the road and in the same direction that we were moving. I noticed that we were getting closer to the side of the road and the next thing I knew we were heading for the woods! I looked at Pep. He was just waking up! He jerked the steering wheel to the left.

"Oooh," he said, sucking in air, and then to the right, "ahh, ahhh." He sounded desperate, frightened, steering left and right again, trying to regain control. The car was bouncing all around, and I was holding onto the dashboard. No seat belts back then. We came to a rocking stop, and a cloud of dust settled over the car. It was quiet except for Mr. Sawyer who kept saying, "Jesus Christ, Jesus Christ!"

It had all happened in less than fifteen seconds. Pep was still muttering when he got out to check the car and the boat. I don't recall any damage.

I do recall a change in Pep's demeanor. He pulled me aside, put his hands on my shoulders, and with a serious and scared look on his face, he said, "Don't ever tell anyone about this. Especially your grandmother." His words were orders but his face was that of a supplicant.

I was reluctant to keep secrets from my parents, but I said, "Ok Pep, I won't."

I kept his secret for over twenty years, and then one night when I was visiting my grandparents, I brought it up as a funny and playful story. It started with something like, "Pep, remember when we went fishing in Lake Winnipesaukee..." I told the story, and he was smiling and chuckling as I spoke. Mem wasn't. She found nothing at all amusing about it. Even though it had happened two decades before, she fixed a lethal glare on Pep that didn't release, even as I was going out the door. Whatever was said after I left must not have been pleasant.

I do know that my grandfather had disappointed her in the past. After he died, she sometimes hinted at those disappointments. There were veiled suggestions of possible cheating (I later found out that was untrue) as well as unveiled statements of gambling. He once lost his car in a poker game. He liked his beer but was not an alcoholic.

Like a lot of guys from that time, he was not a great husband as viewed from today's lens. Men were men and expected to act in a certain way and women were expected to understand. He was charming and good natured, and people liked him. Like a lot of women from that era, Mem would have to swallow a bitter pill from time to time and go on with her life. "Boys will be boys" seems to have been accepted as a common excuse for bad behavior.

Even so, Pep and Mem lived their lives together and loved each other in their own way. In some conversations, he would call her a "real pipperoo," an endearment not well understood now, but high praise in their time.

She would laugh, pretend coyness, and say, "Oh George."

VIEW FROM THE SMOKIES
Karen Wagner

"The Smoky Mountains are a rare jewel. Why not have a place where you can still see the stars?"
—James Dawson

On clear days I count
the ridges, imagine the formations
separating plains from coasts, fisherman
from farmers, fishing caps of the Carolina flats
from straw hats of the Tennessee fields.
I mean this to be my occasional retreat.
This soothing scene of what I think
as not mine, but every man's dream,
as they venture here
for a wisp of calm breeze.
Through the gaps in the trees I see
magnificent vistas of Clingman's Dome
to the south, swivel left for Mount Guyot
Mount Le Conte
covered with new blue mist.

Down here in the hollows
where most folks live
common lives—daylilies
one by one—life is slow and primal.
Most never trek
into the bluish misted mountains.
Domain of wild pigs, black bear
bobcats and white-tailed deer.
Why go there, except on a hunt?

Life here is plain. No IT, AI or Apple—
anything except what grows on trees.
Plenty of chickens, goats, geese
patched overalls.
Moonshine for all who ail.
A hard life? Yes.
A little song and dance
and praise to the Lord
smoothes the rough edges.

Still a musical haunt.
Makers of dulcimers and banjos,
just a few miles east of Gatlinburg.
Listen for cloggers in Mason's
Gulch on Saturday nights.
When the dancers pause for a breath
there'll be some local tunes
picked on those strings, singing too.
Contented folks, sensible lives,
not all destined to gather
in the Smokies' clouded heights.

TREASURE RIGHT IN FRONT OF ME
Sharon Ann Harmon

I read the lovely story by Phyllis Cochran of Winchendon in Devotional Stories for Tough Times. Her story, *Treasures in the Attic, Treasures in Heaven,* was a great inspiration to me. Her poignant story about her daughter Susan who had died and how she dealt with some of her personal belongings and also her memories moved me to tears. I had also lost a child, my son Shon, many years after Phyllis had lost her daughter.

Like Phyllis, I treasured every little thing I had left of him. About 13 years after his death I became a grandmother to my first grandchild Sawyer Shon and one year later to his little sister Bailey Shon. I was thrilled that my daughter had named both the children after him. She had been nine years old when her brother died.

After reading Phyllis's story I realized that I could make Shon's memories a part of my grandchildren's life. I would try to tell them stories and would show them pictures of him. When Sawyer got older and was into Star Wars I gave them both Shon's Star Wars sheets and his Mickey Mouse blankets. I also gave him Shon's highly coveted rock collection and have put away his baseball cards until they are older.

Some days I still find it hard to believe he is gone. I have a picture that my daughter had matted and framed for me hanging in the kitchen. It had just been hung when my grandchildren were visiting and sitting on the kitchen island looking at it. "Who is that Grandma? Is that me?" Four-year-old Sawyer asked. I looked at it and then at him and tried hard not to, but I burst into tears. Trying to recover quickly in front of them I said, "That was Shon, he was my little boy."

"Where is he?" Sawyer asked. "He's in heaven with the angels," I said. Sawyer looked at me with his large brown and wise eyes and said, "Well don't cry Grandma you still have me," the words flew straight to my heart. Of course, he was right; God had given me these two beautiful little children to love, although nothing could ever take Shon's place. These two darling children were put here to fill the large void in my heart.

ROADSIDE JEWELS
Les Clark

Don't rush!
They'll still be there.
So many things out by the curb,
While chipmunks wait…hiding.

There, a lonely chair with one arm.
And a once glorious table…leaning.
The leaves collect around their legs
In a red gold autumn skirt.

Cars slow for this silent auction.
It'll be there later, they think.
The next "shopper" has other ideas.
Their trunk plays finders-keepers.

The wind has competition
It did not have before us.
An irritating noisemaker
Makes a cloud of fallen beauty.

The brave and able
Perform the chores of old,
With wood rake and muscle,
Mixing sweat with chilly air.

Red checkered flannel,
Warm covering for hearty work.
A leather cap with shady bill.
It's fall's fashion, summer's farewell.

Night's dark curtain
Brings an end to wasted effort.
A breeze at dusk takes what was there
And returns it to the grassy clearing.

From rock walls
And gaps in stairway brick,
Flashes of brown and slight white bands
Continue the gathering of winter's stores.

The day of rest is not to be.
Clumps of damp soldiers clog,
Needing another place to gather,
Piled high in stiff brown paper.

Out of that ill-lit place
Come new roadside offerings:
A wagon wheel? A note…IT'S FREE.
But not an ancient crimson cart.

Chipped paint. Missing paint.
The "kidnappers" pay no mind.
In fact, they pay so little
But they leave no mess behind.

Out back, where the air is still,
Grey fur stops, eats…stops, eats.
Eyes dart, paws pause.
The escape tree is close.

High above, silent as a feather
An appetite circles,
Eyeing the ground's hide and seek.
A hungry shriek and it's gone.

Meanwhile, another gift is snatched.
And the scrawled note says: THANK YOU!
It's slipped in a weathered fault
Of the weary, grayed fence.

As the warmth of late fall
Slips low across the reddened sky,
Voices fade behind the closing door.
Chimney smoke curlicues away.

Stars sparkle frosty…cold as ice.
Comfort outside is now comfort in.
Bits of straw for some.
Fleece for those who raked.

Soon, banners and tassels of white
Will drape every stick and stone.
The days will end too early,
And leaves will wait 'til spring.

"I DON'T REMEMBER"
Sue Moreines

When they arrived at the guardhouse, Adam and Sarah had to stop and show their IDs before the chain link fence would open to allow them in. Parking as close to the front door as possible, Adam helped his Aunt Sarah from the car, and they walked slowly, arm in arm, into the surprisingly inviting brick building. Once inside, the receptionist showed them to Dr. Wilson's waiting room, furnished with a couch, four armchairs and a long wall covered in doctoral certificates. There were also two new eye-catching prints strategically placed on another. One was of a dark gathering storm, illustrated with trees being twisted by the wind and the presumed rustling of falling leaves. The other revealed a bright, cloud filled sky with a rainbow subtly sketched in the far-right corner. Sarah spent a few minutes looking at each, noting the Russian artist who painted them. She squeezed the handle of her pocketbook as she recognized their significance, doing the best she could to clear deep-seated traumatic memories from her mind.

Dr. Wilson soon appeared, interrupting Sarah's distressing thoughts. His greeting was warm and welcoming, followed by an invitation to enter his office. Sitting in a wheelchair with her legs covered by a crocheted blanket was someone Sarah and Adam knew well. Three chairs had been set up across from her, and everyone took a seat.

The woman in the wheelchair didn't raise her head until Dr. Wilson said, "Our guests are here, Mrs. Shapiro. As a reminder, today's plan is to review how you've been doing, share information, and answer questions. I'll be taking notes."

Mrs. Shapiro looked blankly at the three faces watching her. Then she shrugged her shoulders and pulled at the white, blue, and red afghan on her lap. Sarah's heart sank, knowing what was going to happen next.

Dr. Wilson pointed toward the man sitting next to him and asked, "Do you know who this is, Mrs. Shapiro?"

"No. Who is he?" she replied.

"He's your son, Adam," he answered.

The smile on Adam's face faded as a loud sigh left his lips. Sarah reached over and held onto his trembling knee.

The doctor then gestured to the person sitting beside Adam. "How about this lady?"

"No! Why do you keep asking me about people I've never met before?" uttered Mrs. Shapiro angrily.

"She's your sister, Sarah. Sarah Abrams," he added.

Sarah had been dreading the day Esther no longer recognized her. She often imagined what it might be like, but none of that made the inevitable any less painful.

"Esther, please! Please try harder. Are you sure I don't look familiar?" pleaded Sarah.

Esther bowed her head, fidgeted, and adjusted her blanket before looking up and saying, "Let me tell you what I do know. Somehow, I ended up in this place. In fact, it's quite nice. I don't have to cook, clean, or wash my clothes. Every day, there's something new and enjoyable to do, so I'm never bored or lonely."

"I'm so glad to hear that, Mom," said Adam. "But, it's hard to accept that you don't remember us. You've been here for a long time and after Dad died last year, I haven't been the same. Missing you and losing him has been devastating. Not knowing why you're here, or what life was like when you lived at home doesn't matter anymore. I love you just the same."

"I'm sorry, but I don't know what you're talking about," replied Mrs. Shapiro.

Adam did his best to hold it together, but couldn't stop himself from hyperventilating and clenching his fists.

"And that breaks my heart," Sarah said, putting her arm around Adam's shoulders. "Every night I think about you and reminisce about growing up. We shared a canopy bed, fought over what to listen to on the radio, and played skully with Ricky, Margaret, and Ernest. I still think we had the best collection of bottle caps filled with colorful melted crayons."

Adam was finally able to regain his composure, and when Sarah finished talking he looked at his mother and said, "I have so many special memories of you, Dad and Eric. But, you and Aunt Sarah are the only family I have left."

Anticipating what Adam was about to say next, Sarah interjected, "As Adam explained, losing someone you love can be terribly hard to deal with. That's especially true if it's your child."

"Or your brother," Adam added. "Eric died on 9-11, and for me, it's been a nightmare. I wish I could erase the flashbacks and reality of what happened that day."

Mrs. Shapiro looked puzzled and began to fidget in her chair.

"This is why we have monthly family meetings, Mrs. Shapiro," said Dr. Wilson. "People with dementia experience memory loss, but they can sometimes remember important things that occurred in their past. It's important to monitor how your dementia is progressing, so we can provide the best care for you."

"What are you talking about? I don't have dementia, whatever that is," she growled.

"You're right, mom," replied Adam. "All that matters is for you to be happy and healthy. The staff here make sure your needs are met, and we don't worry about your safety anymore."

"I still don't know why you keep calling me mom, but I'm glad you can see I'm doing just fine," she answered.

"But it's challenging at our age, Esther," began Sarah. "There aren't many friends or family left to talk with, and we certainly can't do the crazy things we did as kids. I'm grateful Adam and I have remained close, and I try to be the best mother figure possible, despite the fact he's a grown man. You raised an amazing son, Esther and if you're able to retrieve memories of him, you should feel very proud."

Dr. Wilson had been listening closely to the conversation, and then asked an open-ended question, "What happened to your parents, Mrs. Abrams?"

"Well, after we moved to New York, mom and dad worked long hours in a grocery store to support us. Esther and I adjusted well and were fortunate to be able to go to school, have friends and enjoy life. I suppose you could say we were a normal family who did our best during trying times. Despite their busy work schedule, our parents always made time for family dinners and holiday celebrations. We listened to many stories about what life was like in the old country. Some things were hard to hear, and Esther and I didn't always believe what we were told, at least until we were in high school and learned about Russia, Germany and the Holocaust.

Our parents lived well into their 90s and passed away within months of one another. They were rarely apart, so we took solace in knowing they were reunited in death."

Mrs. Shapiro grasped the armrests and became increasingly agitated. Dr. Wilson got up, turned the wheelchair around, and quietly said, "Listening to certain conversations sometimes makes us anxious, but taking a few deep breaths and a break often helps." Mrs. Shapiro responded well to the doctor's suggestion, and was able to work on calming herself down by humming a tune.

Sarah and Adam moved to the back of the room to do the same, but as they returned to their seats, it was obvious they were still uneasy. Dr. Wilson suggested consideration be given to ending the meeting early, but Sarah said they wanted to continue. Mrs. Shapiro even seemed to tilt her head in agreement.

Closely monitoring everyone's demeanor, Dr. Wilson was comfortable allowing the visit to proceed. During Mrs. Shapiro's extended stay at the facility, each family session covered a variety of topics, rarely resulting in notable emotional distress. However, today was progressing differently, so Dr. Wilson remained vigilant.

"Mrs. Abrams, I was wondering if there was something important you wanted to tell Mrs. Shapiro?" guided the doctor.

"In fact, there is," she responded.

"Esther, even though Adam has always been reserved and shy, he suggested we share something with you today, hoping it might awaken some pleasant memories. I was surprised he came up with the idea, and since I'm outspoken and excitable, I jumped up and down in my seat and agreed with him. Of course, Adam preferred that I fill you in on the back-story, unless he's changed his mind," Sarah wondered, looking in Adam's direction.

"You do the talking, Aunt Sarah, and I'll take care of the important part," said Adam.

"That's a fair deal," she answered. "I invited Adam over for dinner last night, and as usual, we took many trips down memory lane. I laid out the photo albums, and we laughed and cried for hours. Then, Adam said he had a very special gift for me, as he looked to his left."

That was Adam's cue to slide his hand into his pocket and bring out his cell phone. After pushing a few buttons, the sound of

"Stardust" by Hoagy Carmichael filled the room. Esther immediately began to tap her feet and Sarah sang along with a song that reminded her of childhood. Even Dr. Wilson smiled as he watched their eye contact and Esther's nonverbal expression of pleasure.

When the music stopped, Sarah exclaimed, "That was such a magical time for us. We shared our hopes and dreams for the future, and to our amazement, many of them came true. You became a teacher, probably because you were giving, respectful and practical and I worked at the Museum of Modern Art as a curator. Life was good to us."

Esther never looked away from her sister, and her eyes opened wide when Sarah reached into her handbag and pulled out an old, well-worn white handkerchief. Placing it in the palm of her hand and stretching out her arms Sarah said, "This was Dad's, Esther. Do you remember?"

Esther stared deeply into Sarah's blue eyes and didn't make a sound. After an uneasy amount of time, Esther dropped her head down, tugged at her hair and spoke quietly in Russian.

After a few moments Dr. Wilson asked, "Is there something wrong, Mrs. Shapiro?"

Letting her arms fall gently into her lap, Esther slowly lifted her head, looked back at Sarah and said, "Before we escaped, life was hell."

Adam's heart skipped a beat, Dr. Wilson leaned forward in his chair and Sarah began to shake. Esther had closed her eyes and resumed humming while tightly gripping the armrests on her wheelchair.

Before Dr. Wilson was able to intervene, a tear rolled slowly down Esther's wrinkled cheek as she opened her eyes, looked back at Sarah and said, "We were hunted like animals, and if our grandparents hadn't hidden us in a crawl space under the floorboards, we would have been shot too. Dad covered my mouth with that hankie so I wouldn't scream, and mom held you tight against her chest."

Sarah tried not to wail, while screaming, "Stop, Esther! No more! I don't want to relive that part of our lives. It was bad enough seeing the artwork in Dr. Wilson's waiting room. I only wanted to see if you remembered Dad!"

"How horrible!" said Adam. "I never knew any of this, and I'm so glad I didn't. Now I'm going to have that memory burned into my brain too."

Esther remained silent while Sarah sobbed, covered her ears, shook her head from side to side, and repeatedly gasped for breath. Adam did his best to console his aunt, and Dr. Wilson seemed to be at a loss for words.

Sarah soon realized what she had done. In an apologetic voice she said, "I'm so sorry I did that, Esther, for all of us. I never expected you to remember that agonizing piece of our history. I only hoped we might reminisce about Dad.

Esther replied, "Sarah, no matter how hard I've tried to permanently free myself from the horrifying part of our past, at times it continues to haunt me. I don't remember much of what happened after we crawled under the barbed wire fence at the Russian border and it still feels like a miracle we got out. Despite immigrating to the United States as children, our painful roots have followed us. That's why living in the here and now is a blessing. Wouldn't you agree, Sarah?"

Adam shook his head in agreement and Dr. Wilson closed his notepad.

CITY SNAPSHOT
Lorri Ventura

A minefield of homeless people
Strewn like pickup sticks
Across the pavement
On the brick and concrete sidewalks
Of Central Square

Shoppers zigzag around them
With their eyes locked on their cell phones
To avoid truly seeing
Those less fortunate

Cocooned in layers of raggedy cardigans
A spavined woman sprawls along a bench
Clutching the matted fur
Of a pumpkin-colored cat
Curled, Cheeto-like,
Against her torso

A bearded man
Lost in billowing, cookie dough camouflage pants
Lurches forward in a wheelchair
That seems to be held together
By bumper stickers

He extends a coffee-stained paper cup
Toward passersby
Hoping for charity
Chuckling, he points to the largest decal
Its message:
"So many pedestrians, so little time."

A trio of laughing college students
Engrossed in conversation
Trample on a potholder-crocheted afghan
That a young girl has spread out on the sidewalk
To define the boundaries of her "home"

Spitting profanities
She glares up at the oblivious trespassers
Her peers in age if not in fortune
And brusquely swats at the footprints
Left on her most precious possession
Dickensian scenes in the 21st century
Mock our claims of social enlightenment
Expose our lack of humaneness
And beg us all to wake up

SHOULD I RETURN AGAIN?
Molly Chambers

Return to the now empty lot where once
Stood the family home filled with love and
Laughter, the sound of trains clacking
Across the street.
Return to the empty places of your
Father, your mother, your brothers and
Your sister;
Family, the rock that held it all up.
Return to the memories of family
Dinners cooking, new babies crying,
Sharing stories,
Laughter from the kitchen and
Church music and Dr. King
On the radio.
Return to the church down the street
Where the pastor's words echoed,
White-clothed ladies comforted and
Hymns of praise rang out.
Return to the stoop sitting grandfather
Watching over his grands, the smell of
Apple pie baking, fried chicken crackling,
And greens and sweets bubbling.
Return to the first house we shared, the
First garden we planted, the first walls
We painted and the first bed we shared.
Now, the memories only remain in the
Corners of our mind and we are blessed.

SWIFT RIVER SECRETS
J. A. McIntosh

This is an excerpt from the novel "Swift River Secrets." Emma Wetherby, the archivist at the Swift River Valley Historical Society, discovered the body of a docent, Grace Connelly. The police investigate and Emma's partner, Todd Mitchell, the police chief, takes her home. This scene starts as they leave.

We were both silent until we got to the car. Todd kept his arm around me, though I assured him that my dizziness had passed. He got into the driver's seat and started the ignition.

"Thank you for getting me out of there." I fastened my seatbelt. "I can't wait to get home, take a hot bath, and go to bed."

"We're having dinner tonight with Brian and Dierdre." He put the car in drive and we started off down the road. "What are we going to feed them? Or do you want to go out?"

"Oh, shit. I'd forgotten about them. Can we postpone it?"

Todd turned to stare at me. It was a rural road, we were the only people on it, but still. "Keep your eyes on the road."

"They said they wanted to talk to us about something important," Todd said.

He was right, those were almost their exact words. I didn't want to do this, but they were Todd's kids. Well, Dierdre was his daughter and Brian was his step-son, child of his former wife, Carol. Todd had enough issues with starting another family when his first two children were adults, without my canceling this dinner that had taken weeks to set up. I'd planned to get home early and do a pork roast, one of Brian's favorite dishes. It was still in the freezer. Why did I have to be in charge of everything?

"I don't feel like getting dressed up and going out." My first line of defense was always addressing only the question Todd asked. "Let's stop at the general store and see what they have. It's not pizza night, is it?"

"Pizza night is Friday. Not today."

Todd's first line of defense was stating the obvious.

"And don't tell them about the pregnancy," Todd added.

We'd been through this discussion before. I had a medical appointment tomorrow; it would be the first time he came with me.

He insisted we not tell his children until afterward. I know I'm pregnant and saw no point in pretending I wasn't.

Todd reached across the console to take my hand. "I know you've had a rough day. And I know I'm sometimes difficult to live with. But thanks for doing this."

"They're going to know before long. My clothes are getting tight."

"I just want the time to be right. They have something important to tell us, let's just concentrate on that tonight." Todd pulled into the parking lot of the New Salem Country Store.

That might be the best plan. Other than family gatherings and holidays, this was the first time I remembered them asking for a family meeting to discuss something. We went into the store, where the smell of corn chowder permeated the room. We bought a gallon (it was good leftover), some bread and salad fixings. Todd checked out the bakery and got a chocolate cake for dessert; it was a favorite of his and of Brian's.

"I need to tell them about what happened at the historical society. About Grace."

"Why?" asked Todd. "Can't we just have a pleasant evening?"

"Todd, I found a dead body today. The first dead body I've ever seen, other than on satin during calling hours. And I'm pregnant and keeping it a secret. Brian is a little dense, like you, but Dierdre will wonder why I'm an emotional mess. They need an explanation."

"Does it make you feel better to call me dense?"

"Yes, it does." I smiled, the first time in hours. "And thank you for not making me elaborate on the dead body." I blinked away the tears. Not here and now.

We got home about a half hour before the children were expected. They weren't children, but I called them that because Todd did. My own personal statement, as I was only nine years older than Brian. Barney, the wonder dog, greeted us at the door. I gave him fresh water and fed him supper. He went to flop in the corner. Todd said he would take care of the food while I went to lie down for a few minutes and get myself together. Before I left, I reminded Todd that Barney would need to be put in the shed; he had a dog bed there for when Dierdre came to visit. She was allergic to dogs and Barney shed lots of hair.

The slamming of the door and footsteps let me know that our visitors had arrived. I put on some mascara and lip gloss and checked myself in the mirror. As I came down the stairs, I heard Todd telling Brian and Dierdre that I wasn't feeling well. He said I'd found a body that afternoon at the society and it had taken a lot out of me. No mention of my pregnancy. I saw no reason to keep it a secret, but Todd wanted to wait to tell his children. Though after today, it would probably be the talk of the town. I hope he didn't wait too long.

I entered the kitchen, where the three of them had gathered. "I'm feeling much better now. Do you need help with the meal?"

All three turned to look at me. Todd had a wine bottle in his hand and three glasses on the counter.

"Dad was just pouring wine," said Brian. "Do you want some?" He got up and took another glass out of the cupboard.

"None for me," I said.

"Me neither," said Dierdre. She turned to me. "Are you sure? It will calm your nerves."

But it probably wouldn't do much for the baby. The baby we weren't talking about. "I'll just have seltzer water. It'll settle my stomach."

"Dad was telling us what happened to you," said Dierdre. "Was it awful?" She shook her head and waved her hand. "That's not what I meant. I'm sure it was awful. Are you sure you're up to having us here?"

This was my chance to cut the evening short, to go back upstairs and just lay on the bed and stare at the ceiling. "No, it's fine. I have to eat anyway, and I want to hear your big news."

Todd filled two glasses and we took them into the living room. Brian and Dierdre sat on the loveseat together and Todd and I took the arm chairs. Nobody seemed to want to start the conversation.

"Are you going to be investigating the murder at the museum?" Dierdre asked.

"Not likely," said Todd. "Emma found the body and that means I have a conflict."

"Something finally happens in New Salem and you don't get to be a part of it?" Brian stopped talking and looked at the floor. "That sounds horrible, I know. Do you know the woman who died?"

"She's a docent at the museum. Emma knows her," Todd said. "I went to school with her, but haven't seen her for years."

"Can we talk about something else?" I asked.

Todd took it upon himself to change the topic. "Tell us how you've been doing. Now that both of you are living in Boston. Do you see each other regularly?"

"That's what we came out to talk to you about," said Brian. "Our plans."

"You're making plans together?" Todd took a sip of wine. "I thought you were taking water samples and Dierdre was selling pastries."

The two of them looked at each other, then down at the floor. Brian was an environmental engineer; he did significantly more than take water samples. Dierdre sold software and social media services to restaurants, bars, and bakeries. Todd often downplayed their jobs and education, but neither of them had ever looked uncomfortable with his teasing before.

"Dad, you know we both have good jobs." Brian reached out and took Dierdre's hand. "We both make more than you do."

Now it was Todd's turn to look at the floor. Not that Brian's statement wasn't true.

"I have an important job," said Todd. "Even if I don't get a chance to investigate Grace's death."

"We know," said Brian. "But what we do is important too. And we're making plans for the future."

"What plans?" asked Todd. "Either of you in a relationship? Going to make me a grandfather?" Todd sipped the wine. "Of course, I'm way too young to be a grandpa."

I looked at Todd, hoping for him to announce my pregnancy. My mouth opened, then closed. These were his kids, he needed to do it on his time. Todd remained silent.

"That's what we want to talk to you about," said Dierdre.

"You're getting married." Todd leaned forward into his seat. "You've met the love of your life."

"Not like you think," said Dierdre.

"Nothing's going like I think," said Todd. "Just today, I've been at the scene of a murder and found Emma right in the middle of it. I'd looked forward to a dinner with you two. What's going on?"

"We didn't come here for the food," said Brian. "We came to see you."

"I know that." Todd put his wine glass on the side table. "But it's been a day of surprises. Tell me yours."

Brian moved closer to Dierdre, though they were both jammed on the love seat. "Dierdre and I are getting married."

The silence piled up in the corners. Todd leaned back in his chair, staring at his daughter and his stepson.

Brian took Dierdre's hand, already in his, and pulled it onto his lap. "We've been attracted to each other since high school," he said. "But this last year, we realized we wanted to stay together forever."

"But you're brother and sister. Siblings don't get married," Todd said.

I wasn't sure this was the right thing to say, but I kind of agreed with Todd. Brian and Dierdre had been twelve years old when Todd married Brian's mother, so they had grown up together. I thought about my feelings for my brother; romance was never a part of our relationship. He was my biological brother, but still, this bothered me.

"We're not siblings," said Brian. "And we are going to get married."

"When is the wedding?" I asked. They struck me as the type of couple that would want a huge blowout wedding, one that would take a year or more to plan. Lots could happen in a year.

Todd got up, went into the kitchen, and came back with the rest of the bottle of wine.

I saw black dots before my eyes. My pregnant body was betraying me again.

"Let's talk about this," I said. "What plans have you made?"

"Emma, are you alright?" Dierdre got up and came over to stand by me. "You're awfully pale and you slurred your words."

"It must be a delayed reaction to the murder," I said. "It's thrown me off my game." I glared at Todd, willing him to say something. He ignored me. "Tell me about your plans."

"We've put a deposit down on a house," said Dierdre. "We're supposed to close at the end of May."

Whoa. That sounded permanent and committed. Todd still hadn't said anything and was staring at the wine in his glass. Like he was trying to decide whether to drink it or to strangle Brian.

"Buying a house," said Todd. "That sounds serious."

"We are serious," said Dierdre. "And we're planning to get married in July."

"July of this year?" Todd started pacing back and forth across the living room. Eight steps and turn. Eight steps and turn. Our living room wasn't that large. "Why the rush?"

Dierdre took a deep breath and let it out with an audible sigh. In an ominous moment, I knew what was coming next.

"Dad," said Dierdre. "I'm pregnant."

Todd stopped pacing. "And it's Brian's kid?" He had on his "cop face," the one that shut out the world. Never play poker with him.

"Of course it's mine," said Brian. "We're going to be parents in November. How could you even ask that, after what we've told you?"

One month after I was due. Todd would have a grandchild just one month younger than his child. He'd be a pop-grandpop. I muffled a giggle that escaped before I could stop it.

Todd turned to me. "You think this is funny?"

I didn't say anything. I wanted to get up and move around but was afraid my legs wouldn't support me.

"I wanted you to know first, before we told anyone else," said Dierdre. "There's a whole part of our life that we haven't let you see, and I wanted it to stop. Don't you think we should share the big events in our life?"

"You told me first? You haven't told your mother?" Todd stopped pacing and confronted Brian.

Brian stood up. "Of course we told mother. She was the first, but you are a close second. I hope you are happy for us."

"I need to talk to Carol." Todd put down his glass and looked around, as if he were going to call Carol, Brian's mother, immediately. "What did she say about your plans?"

"She's happy for us," said Dierdre. "It's difficult to find someone special and, with Brian, we've already worked out the living together part."

"As brother and sister," said Todd. "Not as a married couple. And not as parents."

"Mom is happy for us. Why can't you be too?" This from Dierdre, who looked anxiously from Todd to Brian.

"It's a lot to take in," said Todd. "I've always thought of you as my children, but now it's a whole other experience. I thought families shared things."

That was the surprising subtext of this conversation. We knew about the events in their lives, but Todd still didn't share the news of my pregnancy. He made a fist with both hands and held them at his side. He was trying hard not to say what he was thinking. He resumed pacing.

"I've barely gotten used to the idea that you are both adults, now I'm going to be a grandfather," said Todd. "Double."

"Excuse me." I hurried out of the room and barely made it to the toilet before getting sick. Good thing I'd only had seltzer water. I sat on the toilet seat and waited for the dizziness to pass.

When I returned to the living room, Dierdre and Brian had their coats on. "Aren't you staying for dinner?" I pointed to the food, set out on the table.

"No," said Brian. "I think we should leave. Give you a chance to think about what was obviously a shock to you."

Dierdre went over to Todd and put her hand on his arm. "Once, you said that you would love me no matter what I did. I hope that's still true."

Todd threw back his shoulders and stared past Dierdre's head. He didn't say anything.

I walked to the door with them. "I'll call you," I said. "We can work this out. I'm sure your father will come around."

Todd continued to stand and stare as they left the house.

The car started and drove away.

"You should've told them you loved them," I said.

BELOVED SON, MOUNTAIN MAN NED

Clare Green

Is it any wonder, you,
Perished from that Mountain,
From the state of New Hampshire,
"Live Free or Die," its motto?

You had a choice didn't you?
But you were brave enough to let go, to be free,
Knowing your "ole ma" would be okay.
You stepped aside, so your

Climbing partner could safely reach summit,
An ice damn released, and you,
Cascaded 800 feet from Damnation Gulley
Ha! You, the poet, would love that irony.

An eclipse of my heart,
Yet love never dies, sorrow transforms
Shock of spirit and washing bloodied clothes at the sink,
Days later, you, garbed in light, stood by my side.

Is it any wonder, you,
At birth, stopped breathing, but then,
Inhaled again, bringing years of joy and story,
To your mother and father?

Cuddly baby to athlete and hard worker,
Potter, poet, composter, hiker, climber, baker
And in your College of Atlantic Yearbook,
A lone inscription, "I Worship Mountains."

Is it any wonder, you,
Arrived atop Mt. Washington at three weeks of age,
Then bid adieu 26 years later, from the same mountain,
As Caretaker #2 of Harvard Mountaineering Club Cabin.

Is it any wonder that these circles of comfort
Breathed order and destiny,
From lifetimes of gnarled roots and sprouts,
Into profound gratitude filled to overflowing?

Yes, live free or die, no wonder.

Grass Roots

"INTERNAL ROOTS"
DIANE KANE

MR. PIPER, HERMIT ON A HILLTOP
Phyllis Cochran

Mr. Piper moved into our neighborhood in 1948. As a young girl, roots from the ordinary ran deep. I thought of this man like a character in a novel. He taught me a lesson that I would carry with me for the rest of my life.

Adults referred to him as Raw Piper, a harmless eccentric man. We kids, tagged him 'a hermit' because he stayed to himself and always hiked through the woods when running errands.

When he showed up on Brown Street in our neighborhood as he seldom did, I studied him from a distance. He was a tall, lean man, walked with a bounce in his step and always carried a stick. In winter and even on the hottest summer days, he wore a black hat, jacket, and hiking boots and mumbled as he passed.

I wondered about Mr. Piper's shack on the hilltop and was leery about his German Shepherd. His property was loaded with the largest, most juicy, high-bush, blueberries that I had ever seen. Our motley group gravitated there to pick berries. We learned to watch for his dog tied outside. This usually meant Mr. Piper was home, otherwise the dog would be inside. Although he never threatened anyone, I was apprehensive of how he might react if he caught us on his land. We tried to remain on guard should he show up and chase us away.

One afternoon we sneaked onto the edge of his property and were busily filling our containers with berries when he appeared like an apparition before us. We had nowhere to run or hide. He stood blocking the road. Instead of chasing us, he said, "There are more high bush blueberries further up. Follow me."

For the first time, I realized Mr. Piper could speak. Obediently, we followed from a distance toward his house where berries draped in clumps like grapes. Afterwards, he invited us into his home. We stepped onto wobbly planks before entering his one-room shanty.

"He won't hurt you," he said, pointing to his dog. "Have a seat." We crowded together on a musty smelling sofa. I glanced around. Unlike our modest home, dirty dishes filled the sink. It looked as though the place hadn't seen a broom or dust cloth for months.

"I know where there are lots more berries," he told us. "I can take you to Big Rock, but it's quite a long way into the woods."

We hurried home to get our parents' permission for the excursion on that hot summer afternoon. Four or five of us kids trudged along behind our guide. Grass had been trampled down on the pathway probably by Mr. Piper himself.

After a lengthy trek through the woods, we reached a clearing. Dropping our buckets, we dashed over and scrambled up on top of Big Rock. Forgetting the berries, we giggled and swatted mosquitoes.

Mr. Piper enticed us down by promising to find a stream of cool spring water where we could quench our thirst. He procured a rusty cup hidden beneath some bushes, filled the goblet, and offered us a refreshing drink. When my turn came, I peered down past the corroded cup and swallowed.

As we waded in the stream, Mr. Piper told us about the sun and moon. He pointed toward the clear blue sky and began teaching us the position in the Heavens where the stars form the Big and Little Dipper when the sun sets.

Occasionally, over the years a fond remembrance of this afternoon spent with Mr. Piper flashed through my mind, and I shared this memory with friends.

Today his face evades me, blended with the countless people who have crossed my path. He is a faceless and ageless man. He is no longer a mystery or oddity to me. My memory of that afternoon will never fade. That day Mr. Piper shed his facade, and I, the image of the peculiar man I created in my mind. An intelligent and caring human being captured my attention, met us kids on our level, and taught us a few lessons.

It was the only time I spent time with him, but I acknowledged Mr. Piper whenever he walked up our street. He carried on with his life and we with ours.

He may not have realized it, but he taught me an important lesson that afternoon. Although our roots may be different, I learned to look beyond outer appearances and to accept people for who they are behind their masks.

A previous version was published in *Tapestries* at MWCC in 2003

ROOTS IN WINTER

Lisa Lindstrom

Another winter night approaches…the
season of retreat. A hush advances as the
sun retires behind the hills. This night's full
moon will cast its pearlescent silk upon the
land.
A thick snow coats the ground shielding
the cold, slowed life that waits beneath. All
who burrow have evaded the threat of
bitter chill and rooted themselves, deeply,
to the earth.
In time, the warm morning sun will soften
winter's rigidity and spring's valor will
return.
But for now, dreaming birds snuggle
closely together in tree cavities away from
desirous predators.
Beavers, foxes and cottontails engage in
focused nocturnal labors.
Soon I will slip beneath my quilt and
exchange lively wakefulness for a slumber
that divides dusk from dawn.
By the light of the moon unmarked time
passes. An owl hoots and coyotes cry.
A blanket lays across my shoulders. In this
moment I sit comfortably. With each cycle
of breath, thoughts and emotions rise and
fall. Watchfulness reveals a rooted depth
of inner silence. As sleep comes I wonder
at the enduring forces which keep us in
nature's play.

MY GRANDFATHER'S TREE
Steven Michaels

Twisted gnarled fingers entrenched in soil
ground the sycamore
in my grandfather's garden.
How often have I sat under its limbs
readjusting my rump
over the knotted bumps
in search of a comfortable position?
How often have I slid my palms over its roots
prodding my fingers
into the jagged holes
of each insect's burrowing?
These moments seem uncountable
as so many of my lazy youthful days
were spent about the tree.
I've often wondered how old the tree must be.
It's wide enough to have over ninety rings.
To think it was once a sapling
in the years before
my grandfather's birth.
I remember
my grandfather's twisted gnarled fingers.
I remember
how hard he, too, worked in soil.
I remember
how his backside ached
as he readjusted himself in his easy chair.
I remember
how the oxygen tubes
burrowed into him
helping his body
exterminate the parasites within.
Thankfully the tree remains
as do all my memories.
And I remain grateful for the lazy days
that he granted me
in his yard
under his tree.

SWEAT LODGE EXPERIENCE
Clare Green

It was the late 1970s. The idealism and freedom of the 1960s fermented the yearning for spiritual integrity, as a "back to the land" approach to life developed among folks living in the Western Hills of Massachusetts. The vision and hope for a peaceful and spiritual future lay in the remembrance of our indigenous ancestors and how they communed with nature. Cleansing and purifying oneself through sweat lodges and fastings were integral to the natural process of identifying with one's spiritual roots. I thought that to experience a sweat within a natural environment would be so relaxing and inspiring, compared to the Athol YMCA Sauna or the Athol Steam Baths.

A friend of mine invited me to his recently built sweat lodge which was located in the woods, and near a running stream. Perfect. The heat from the steaming rocks nestled within the lodge would be felt, then the natural cool down with a dip into the stream would be ideal. It was planned for a fall afternoon while my young son attended The Giving Tree Preschool in Gill. I would have enough time for the sweat and then be able to pick him up on time.

It would be just the two of us for the sweat. My friend arrived earlier in the day to prep the lodge and start the fire. I bowed when I entered the lodge and readied my space. Silent prayers were said, and there was an honoring to the four directions. My friend chanted, and I sat in meditation inside the lodge as sweat poured from me. Time passed. I felt ready to exit the lodge. As I did, I apparently passed out and my friend stayed near me until I recovered and came to consciousness.

As I opened my eyes, all I saw was scintillating rainbow light. Even my body was completely sparkling rainbows. It was astonishing to see all of life vibrating and emanating as pure sparkling energy: the rock, the trees, the ground, everything! I felt amazed and awed by the beauty.

Slowly my vision returned to the natural world of physical forms, but I was reminded of the Oneness of all creation and the pure energy of light which courses through all of us, like warm sunshine. I was not expecting a vision, but a gift came my way.

Before I returned to my body, I remember having an aerial color vision of my son playing outdoors on the hillside and climbing apparatus at his school. That out-of-the-body experience may have been the signal I needed to help me return more fully to the earth dimension. Later, I was reminded of how many guardians and angels may attend to us unawares.

My friend was glad to see me recovered and more fully present in the body again. Soon, I was grounded enough to drive my car to my son's school and pick him up. The memory of that profound sweat experience has been rooted in my heart, lasting a lifetime.

DAUGHTER
Kersti Slowik

Someday when she starts walking
We'll take her to Story Land,
We'll eat ice cream and ride the teacups
Holding tight to her small, dimpled hand.

Someday when she's in preschool
She'll make friends and learn to share,
She'll sing sweet rhymes and finger paint,
Wearing pigtails in her hair.

Someday when she's in grammar school
She'll pick dandelion bouquets,
She'll wear pink and purple tutus,
Try gymnastics and ballet.

Someday when she's in middle school
She'll grow taller than her mom,
She'll do dance and learn piano,
Each recital, a challenging song.

Someday when she's in high school
The arts will be her passion,
Choir, voice lessons, musicals,
Sound design and quirky fashion.

Someday when she turns sixteen
She'll get a job and learn to drive,
She'll think about college and a career
Where she can truly thrive.

Someday she'll move away from home
Sooner than we'd care to admit,
So we'll live in the moment and savor each day,
For right now, she's still ours for a bit.

So embrace what you've got while you have it,
Every day is a gift from above.
We only have so many "somedays" in life
To share with the ones that we love.

RESILIENCE
Heidi Larsen

Mistakes are fertilizer
To our future growth,
Stimulating perseverance,
Watering creativity,
Pushing our roots deeper
Into the soil;
So that our footing
May be secure and rooted
And our rise is sure.
Hurts will heal in time.
Failures will be forgotten.
What remains behind
Are rich reminders
Of the upward climb,
Drenched with storms and downpours;
Knowing that through the roughest
Rain and the wildest wind
One does grow stronger
And becomes more wise,
Because one has learned
The meaning of the word
Resiliency.

ROOTED IN LOVE
Deb Patryn

My father-in-law, Alec Patryn, was a master carpenter even though he never took a carpentry class. He had built his own home in Dalton, Massachusetts back in the 1950s and then a playhouse for his youngest daughter in the 1960s.

When my daughters, Julie and Amy, were born in the 1980s, he decided to build them a special playhouse for our backyard.

This was no ordinary plastic playhouse like you see today. It was constructed all from wood with a ten-foot peaked roof, two windows on the sides that opened, a double-wide front door, and even a front porch with white railings. It looked like a miniature Swiss Chalet. Alec did not follow plans to build it; he thought it all out himself.

Inside it was tall enough for adults to stand in although they had to duck through the door. He built shelves on the back wall and bought a child-size refrigerator and stove for it. Also inside were a table and chair set that had been mine as a child.

He built the playhouse in his backyard in Dalton, Massachusetts, and he had to load it on a trailer to tow it to our house in Feeding Hills about fifty miles away. Then he traveled with my mother-in-law, Gloria, in the middle of the night to avoid traffic or curious police officers.

My girls were thrilled when they woke up and saw a playhouse in their backyard. After it was situated, the roof needed to be shingled and a painted wooden chimney attached to the roof.

All the neighborhood kids loved coming to our yard to play in the playhouse. It was well-loved for many years until we moved to Southwick, Massachusetts, and sadly had to leave it behind. The girls had outgrown it by then but were still sad to say goodbye.

For many years we would look for the playhouse when we drove by our old house. Then one day it was no longer there, and we didn't know what happened to it. One day while driving to Connecticut I spotted the house in someone else's backyard. I knew it was my girls' playhouse. It had found a new home and new children to love it.

A tradition continues for a playhouse rooted in love.

GROWN BETWEEN A ROCK AND A HARD PLACE
Alison Clark

Planted where you don't belong
Somehow still holding strong
Overextended to grab ahold
Environment uncontrolled
See the world in a specific way
Of that you're certain, you might say
Opinions planted beyond the ground
Locked in place by another surround
Standing still, like the rock
Imagine it is quite a shock
Difficulties must be led
Still your roots grow and spread
Ideas stem from the heart
Grasping for that fresh start
Perception twists a certain way
Sometimes with a price to pay
Thriving here on your own
All this time you have grown
This survival takes great lengths
May you always have this strength
Break the mold of what's expected
Do what it takes to become connected

MY ABUELO'S TRUCK
Eileen Hernández-Cole

Maybe I once imagined it was a playpen. My cousin spent hours in one, and I was too big to nap in it. Maybe it was the cold metal against my skin, refreshing compared to the heat and humidity of Puerto Rico, where I grew up. Or maybe it was the gold-yellow color of it, scratched up to the metal, like a rusty grapefruit and rind. It wasn't a clean bed. There were always pieces of concrete blocks and tile and sand. My grandfather, *abuelo* (Don Toño to everyone else), was a contractor, but he drove me to school my entire kindergarten and first grade in that Ford beast. Sometimes it would backfire, resulting in some stares, but I loved that truck's dented hood with rounded corners and the scratched-up chrome bumpers that barely shone. It was either from the mid 1960s or older, and I often pretended I was driving my grandmother, *abuela*, to the market down the hill.

On the weekends or after school, I often asked *abuelo*, or one of my aunts or uncles, who were just teenagers at the time, to move the truck under the banyan tree, an aerial root tree that thrived in the space between *abuelo's* homestead and my great-grandmother's house. The trees' long brown braids of roots wrapped around some limbs and hung down close to the land. I had been climbing that tree higher and higher as far as I can remember. Sometimes, I would lay on a limb and watch the breeze move the flowering bushes below until ants tickled my arms with their tarsi, tiny feet. The ground itself was mostly uneven with roots and gravel, so it was safer to climb down.

That is why aubelo's gold-colored truck became so ingrained in my childhood memories. When it was parked close enough to the banyan tree, I soared! Two hands holding on tight to as many roots as my fingers could wrap around, and with my body armor of polyester shorts, a tank top, and worn out flip flops, I would sail through the air. My tangles of sunlit hair flew behind me until I landed into that gold bed. I often scraped my palms and toes, but I never complained. It was exhilarating! That yellow truck and its bed was my launching pad because I dared. I never defied again as much as I did then, not after my world became the hard landscape of the Bronx a few years later.

Now I live 1,700 miles away in the hills of central Massachusetts, and my climbing days are decades old. The memory of the single time my boys were able to climb a tree large enough to hold them lives in my mind as a reminder of the childhood they could have had. I do not regret that the trees in our yard were ornamental and too weak for their jumps and tumbles, or that the lowest branches of the oaks and maples were too far up to reach. And while I wished that the local library had not cut the lower limbs off their beech, I understood and agreed that avoiding lawsuits over broken bones was best.

I still tell my boys these stories because I still feel a sense of grounding by my personal memory of swinging off the banyan tree, which was only possible because while my parents were at work, my grandmother could hardly keep up with me. I ran around and napped in the soft grass veining into the aromatic dark soil no longer seeded for food. I was an adventurer flying through the air by my own strength, until *abuela* told everyone to stop parking the truck so close to that tree. I then had to climb down again or risk a truly clumsy landing.

THE DUCK HUNTER
Joseph E Lorion

He's glad the summer's over,
and looks forward to the fall.
Of all the yearly seasons,
he loves this one most of all.

This time of year brings changes,
and makes his world seem right.
With cool and frosty mornings,
and leaves so bold and bright.

He has but a few days,
to gather and pack his gear,
dig out the canoe and decoys,
and get ready for this year.

The guns are in a cabinet,
to keep away the dust.
all clean and shiny,
and free of any rust.

Opening day has finally come,
and a new hunt will be born.
He'll be out there in his duck blind,
long before the dawn.

As the first few rays of daylight,
peek across the sky,
his heart beats even quicker,
and he keeps a wary eye.

From left he hears a familiar sound,
the approaching of whistling wings.
A sound so soft and gentle,
it's almost like it sings.

Though his eyes are getting old,
and he can't see well at night,
he spots the ducks coming at him,
and he keeps them in his sight.

The shotgun snaps to his shoulder,
two explosions fill the air.
Splashes upon the water,
tell him he shot a pair.

The canoe is cold and frosty,
and he's careful not to slip.
He holds the paddle firmly,
not wanting to lose his grip.

He retrieves his trophies,
and pulls the canoe upon the bank,
Lifts his head towards Heaven
and gives a mighty thanks.

With a grin upon his face,
he loads the gear into the truck.
He'll go and find his friends,
and tell them of his luck.

As the sun gets higher in the sky,
a warmness fills the air.
He turns and leaves the other ducks,
For another hunter to share.

Can you feel the frost upon your face
and smell the gunpowder in the air?
It will never leave my memory,
because I was actually there.

PRINCESS, MORE THAN A CAT
Clare Green

Princess. Our black kitty for eighteen years. Soft, pure black fur with green-golden eyes, affectionately greeted us day and night. She hardly meowed. She was a gentle and royal presence in our lives. Her sister cat, Racer, sadly did not survive the move to Warwick from Wendell. True to her name, as bequeathed by my son, she raced out the door one day, never to return to the homestead. Meanwhile, Princess adjusted to our new home, as an indoor/outdoor cat. She would sleep on the couch and come to the bedroom at 6:00 in the morning to be certain I was up for my work and her morning breakfast. Cat routines and playtimes easily fashioned their way into our lives. Her nickname became "Kittums."

Simply, she touched our lives with love and joy as she frisked about, played with homemade string toys, and relaxed on the couch. I'll always remember how her tail flipped over an Angel Card, as she passed by a small group of us meditating and sitting on the living room floor. Which Angel Card? Why, the only one pictured with a Black Kitty! The Angel Card of Tenderness, of course! Yes, Princess reminded me that tending to pets requires keeping an open and tender heart. That cosmic flick of her tail made me smile that evening.

After years of enjoyment, one sad day I came home from work, and she didn't greet me at the door. Later I found that she died curled up on the floor of my bedroom closet. I had recently taken her to the vet's, and we did everything that we could for her. Her passing happened to coincide with a memorable day. It was December 1, 1999, the first worldwide acknowledgment of World Aids Day. Thankful that my son was home for a visit, he helped dig a hole by the backyard stonewall where the ground was still soft. A welcomed spot for Princess' spirit to rest. An old oak tree provided solace. Mice scampered, chipmunks darted, and squirrels scurried. Gently, we laid her to the ground and felt appreciation for the long, tender and uncomplicated life she shared with us. Our hearts silent with appreciation.

So, for the next three weeks, I still heard the same floorboards creak at 6:00AM, just as if Princess were alive and greeting me for the morning's food and adventure. Indeed, her spirit presence was a comfort to me, as I now adjusted to life without her. How dear of her to be near. One morning I realized that the floorboards ceased to creak. Her transition complete, as I was accepting the finality of her life. Memories are now wedded to photos and remembrances of sharing our life with her, as she helped us to put roots down in our new home town of Warwick. Our home became cozier with her love.

EYE OF THE BIRCH
Alison Clark

A lone seed caught on the wind
Settles into a small nook
A soft spot upon the frozen ground
Take hold in the cold soil
The beginning of a journey
Wait now, patience
With warmth, roots may grow

Break free for survival
Year after year, little by little
As the seasons pass
So will the sun, rain, snow
New leaves arrive like clockwork
Always turning green then yellow
Until the branches reach above

Chickadees build cozy nests
Inhabiting a safe hollow
Hard to see, but surely felt
Babies hatch and sing their love
Praising the ephemeral home
But new wings can fly
Fit for adventure

Graceful bounding squirrels
Scamper branch to branch
Hiding snacks for winter
Likely to become forgotten
The chase of pattering feet
A massage for the tree limbs
Weary from standing tall

A curious labrador approaches
Pausing here a moment
Sniffing circles on the ground
Hunting for secret clues
About who else has visited
Little stories linger
Where trunk meets earth

People pass by, back and forth
Some becoming familiar
As they grow older too
Continuing on their way
To the places, unknown
Watch silently in peace
Not enquiring about beyond

A child picks dandelion clocks
Growing in the tall grass nearby
Blowing wishes all around
A reminder of where we're from
One ending into a beginning
New roots will intertwine
Mirroring symmetry above and below

The golden light of the sun
Sets upon what's out of sight
Even under the dark of night
The eye of the birch
Keeps watch over its home
As far as it can to see
As long as there is a will to stand

LEVITATING

Allan Fournier

Hey bartender, I know you've heard some tales.
Here's another one for you:
I'm on a cloud one foot above the ground.
I'm levitating.

My daughter just got married.
She's in a two-pea pod.
So meant for each other.
I'm levitating.

She got her Mountain View
Dramatic clouds and sun.
Got the love of her life.
I'm levitating.

Her mom handled the logistics:
Where does this go and when?
I've got the love of *my* life.
I'm levitating.

She's got the best of friends.
And her beau Joey, too.
It's so easy to see.
I'm levitating.

Hey Spencer Tracy
Of Father of the Bride fame:
I didn't trip down the aisle!
I'm levitating.

The wedding ceremony:
Jay, Marie, and Joey
Each inhabited by Shakespeare and Robin Williams.
I'm levitating.

New two-person family created.
Reunited families for the first time in a while.
I witnessed the joy in their eyes.
I'm levitating.

I'm a capital "W" Wallflower.
Found social butterfly wings for the occasion.
So many great conversations.
I'm levitating.

Dua Lipa's "Levitating"
DJ played this song we requested.
Good choice!
I'm levitating.

Dreams fulfilled.
Dreams in progress.
Bon voyage, they set off from the shore together.
I'm levitating.

THEY NEVER KNEW
Diane Kane

My husband and I married in 1979. I was twenty-one, and he was twenty-three. The following year, we had our first daughter, Shannon, and two years later, our second, Danielle. There wasn't time to think about the money we didn't have. Tom had a job at a machine shop for minimum wage. I worked as a convenience store clerk for the first year of our marriage. When the children came, I found a night job in a restaurant kitchen.

Tom and I passed like ships in the night. He went off to work in the morning and got home just in time for me to hand off the kids to him as I rushed out the door. He made the kids supper and got them to bed. I came home around midnight. We exchanged a couple of words before we went to bed. I worked weekends and holidays in the restaurant. He entertained the kids by taking them for walks in the woods and letting them fashion his hair with barrettes for hours on end.

On my days off, I would have their friends over to play. All of us mothers were pretty much in the same boat—more bills than money. We swapped kid's clothes as each child outgrew them. We combined our resources on Halloween to have parties with apple dunking and donuts on a string. The kids always had piles of used clothes for pretend dress-ups and impromptu living room stage shows.

In the summer, I would pack a lunch with whatever I could find and take them to the town beach for the morning, making it home just in time to change and run off to work. Our mother's group would watch each other's kids whenever someone needed a hand. Yard sales and thrift shops were our regular stops for the best used Fisher-Price toys and household items.

Our so-called vacations were camping trips in a four-person tent that sometimes never went beyond the backyard.

Our girls were grown and wandered to places far and near, but they always came home to their roots to relax and rest. They confided their concerns on one such visit with their own growing families.

"It's so hard," they said. "We never have any extra money."

Tom and I recalled our lean times.

"We barely got by when you kids were little," I said. "Thank goodness for Hamburger Helper and Mac and Cheese."

"Ya," Tom said, "the bill collectors had to wait for their turns. And the cars were always on their last legs. But we got by."

The girls turned to each other in astonishment.

"We never knew," our youngest daughter said.

"We always thought we were rich," said our firstborn.

"Those were the best of times, weren't they?" Tom turned to me and smiled.

"Yes," I said. "We were rich."

WHISPER

Clare Green

Out the back door
Feet on the woodland path
Alongside Shadow
Our faithful collie
These woods know us

My child's mind still
Breathing joy
Whisper me flowers
Nature's perfume
Soft petals touch beauty

Roadside, garden, field or trail
The world is more beautiful because of you
Say it with flowers
Be the flower
Gentle, tender, caring and true

As a child, walking woods, dreaming, free
Stumbling upon a field of vibrant white
And pink phlox, nearly as tall as I
Ahh, such sweet fragrance filled the air, delicate
Resplendent moment of pure grace

Feet return upon path toward home
Hands now clasped with abundant phlox
Gladly a bouquet for mother

The back screen door opens wide
Into the kitchen we step
Where I'll help set the table for supper
And place the bright flowers,
For her, as a centerpiece surprise

And now years sustain the child
Within, as remembrance ignites love
Of whispered flower melodies
With endless blooms

Intertwining Roots

"RECALLING A MEMORY"
JAMES WYMAN

WHERE THERE IS NO SLEEP
James Thibeault

In the middle of the night, Noah looked around the pristine and spotless kitchen—basking in the moonlight and silence. On many nights, he crept downstairs just to hear nothing. He would put on the electric kettle and have a cup. The perfect moments for him were the intermittent sips of his tea amidst the emptiness. He longed to be fully tangled with the nothingness. Perhaps the sips helped him momentarily snap out of his thoughts. A push and pull between reality and oblivion.

His wife was sleeping upstairs and could sleep through a tornado. When their child Aria was a baby and would cry throughout the night, Noah resented at first how she would never stir. It was such an ordeal to wake her that it was much easier for him just to rock Aria to sleep every night. Together, Noah and Aria would brace each other close and dance around the kitchen—a vibrating shuffle until Aria's active eyes would drop and cease. Then Aria would feel even heavier in his arms, and he would put her back to her cradle. However, even with the task done, Noah could not sleep. A thousand thoughts would be racing, and nothing could quell it enough for his eyes to relax like his child. Noah figured that if he could get Aria to sleep from the midnight strolls in the kitchen, perhaps it would work the same for him.

The habit of staying up during the night continued long after Aria grew out of the crib. It seemed Noah rarely slept anymore. Even when he closed his eyes, thoughts raced around a looping track. He found the best way to confront those thoughts was to embrace them. When staring into the darkness for quite some time, he would finally relax. He was awake but asleep. He was lost but found. A clear contradiction. He could not explain the trance that he put himself in, but he accepted it. A faith toward something. A faith toward nothing.

On the other side of the room, a light glow appeared. Noah put down his tea and walked towards his phone that was charging on the counter. He set his phone to silent, but a new message still activated the bright screen. Curious, he grabbed his phone and looked at it. It was a message from his daughter.

~Still awake?

Even though the glow from the screen bothered his eyes, he still managed to reply.

~Yes. Can't sleep again?

~Why can't I be more like Mom?

~Just relax. Sleep will come.

~Says the one still awake ☺

~Breathe, just like we practiced. Go to bed.

~Love you.

~Love you too.

Noah plugged in his phone again and faced it downward. He resumed his spot in the kitchen and sipped his tea. It was not cold, but not suitable enough. Annoyed, he put it in the microwave and set it to 30 seconds. While the microwave light glowed, the cup rotated. Often, he felt like the cup—slowly spinning beyond his control. There was a pattern to his rotating thoughts, but his mind did not want to accept the movement. All he wanted was stillness. To be silent. He was afraid that his daughter had inherited the same curse. They tried meditation and medication, but often they exchanged the same texts night after night. Perhaps they were meant to constantly spin until—

Beep. The microwave light ceased. The rotation stopped. Only a black box remained. Noah opened the door and stared at the renewed light and steaming cup of tea. Gingerly, he grabbed the cup, closed the door, and sat back down. Feeling the warmth in his hands, for a brief moment, he relaxed his eyes and felt the embrace of sleep. Then, his thoughts erupted—jolting his body awake. His hand released his cup, and it crashed to the ground. The handle snapped and tea pooled on the tile. Softly, he swore and grabbed paper towels on the counter. He figured that the loud noise would at least stir something from his wife, but he heard no thumping from above, no squeaking of the mattress. There were some nights like this where he was envious of his wife. She could instantly die, it seemed, only to be resurrected a few hours later. Sleep felt like death to him. Each night, his wife committed seppuku, and her bravery astounded him. She gladly would draw the sword of sleep and plunge it into her body. If only he were that brave.

After cleaning up the mess and throwing away the chipped mug, he sat back down. Without the comfort of the tea, he stared intently into the black void. His eyes were wide, alert, as though he was scanning for threats. However, he knew there was nothing out there, but he searched regardless. Perhaps, if he stared hard enough, he would see what it was he feared. This inner search he tried on many nights, but nothing had ever emerged. Yet, on this night, he saw for a brief moment, a plant. Startled, he stood up as though it was an intruder. He backed up and grouped along the counter for a kitchen knife. When he found the chef knife, he held it near his nose—ready to strike. When he saw his reflection in the metal, eyes wide in fear, he snapped out of it. He placed the knife back into the block and fought back tears. Would he ever sleep?

Since the morning rays were beginning to show, the window had reflected the plant that sat on the counter. He turned to the real plant, a pothos, and studied its green leaves. Noah read how they flourished with low light. How could it thrive in darkness? He wanted to understand. Perhaps it was the week-long lack of sleep, but whatever the reason, Noah turned the plant over and pulled off the pot. He wanted to dissect it, to understand how it survived. He dug into the soil and studied its roots. They spun in the circle—looping around the pot again and again. The roots had a frame identical to the pot itself. These roots wandered around and around in circles. Still, the plant was beautiful. Embarrassed for the exposed plant, he put the pot back in its spot and set the plant back where it was.

What grows, dies. What dies, endures. Those roots were searching for space for something. Instead, they looped and looped in the dark dirt finding no new avenue. It should be dead. The plant should be choking on its own roots—its tendrils all seeking everywhere and for nowhere. Yet, the plant grows, lives. What lives, endures.

The dawn was beginning to appear, and Noah sat back on his chair. At this point, Noah would be waking his wife, preparing breakfast, or watching something on his phone. However, this time, he stared at the rising sun—its morning glow lighting up the kitchen. He felt the warmth of the morning, then nothing.

His wife found him sound asleep hours later.

SARMAS

Elaine Reardon

At the farm near Harput,
Grandmother carried sarmas
on a donkey, lunch for her grandfather.

> Rice, onions and herbs
> rolled in grape leaves
> eaten hot or cold.

Her family grew cabbages, eggplants,
squash, apples and grapes, a bounty.
Poppies, a crop farmers were forced to grow.

> Grapevines, in garden and myth,
> were woven into oriental carpets
> and climbed to the heavens.

Gram lived through a death march to Aleppo,
became a young arranged-marriage bride to survive,
> allowing travel from Syria to America.

> In our yard, Gram led me to the grapevine,
> explained how to find the tender leaves.
> We carefully chose them one by one.

She steamed our grape leaves
and laid them flat, ready to stuff.
Rice, onions, herbs cooked for filling.

> At the kitchen table I stood on a stool
> with my own plate of grape leaves to stuff,
> apron wrapped around me, a new cook.

She showed me how to roll in the rice,
how to tuck the edges like Cuban cigars,
not too tightly, not too loose. Perfect.

       Stacked in in a pot, with
       a plate on top to hold them,
       they simmered in tomato broth.

MRS. D'ANGELO'S YOUNGEST SON

Mary Anne Kalonas Slack

Growing up, Mrs. Angelo's four sons were altar boys and members of the choir. Well, three of them were. Her youngest, Rusty, the bad boy of the lot, was relieved of his church duties by their pastor when he found the twelve-year-old boy drinking unconsecrated wine with a few friends after Mass. Mrs. D'Angelo had been mortified, of course. She and her husband grounded him for a month, but neighbors reported that he'd been seen climbing out his bedroom window and smoking on the porch roof. His father put Rusty to work in his grocery store, stocking shelves and running errands. Rusty liked earning money and interacting with the customers. The job lasted a year until his father caught him making out in the storeroom with a sixteen-year-old cashier. Rusty had just turned thirteen.

Sister Irene, the principal of Saint Columba High School, called the D'Angelos in for a conference in October of Rusty's freshman year. Mr. D'Angelo had to be at the store, so his wife went alone. After asking about Rusty's three older brothers with a smile on her face, Sister Irene got serious. She told Mrs. D'Angelo in no uncertain terms that if her son continued his present course, they would one day visit him in juvenile hall, and eventually in prison. Mrs. D'Angelo didn't defend him to Sister, just nodded her head as she listened. Before leaving the principal's office, Mrs. D'Angelo told Sister Irene that Rusty was a good boy. She believed that Sister Irene was wrong about him. Mrs. D'Angelo did promise to keep a closer eye on him.

That evening at dinner her husband asked what the principal had wanted.

"Oh, everything's fine," she told him. "Sister was a little concerned about Rusty's grades, but I promised to check his homework more carefully in the future." She looked at her son, who was finishing a plate of pasta in his usual ravenous style. She could tell by the way he looked at her that he knew she was lying. "You will be a little more careful, won't you, dear?"

He returned her gaze and promised to do a better job on his homework.

Rusty's homework did improve a bit, but his behavior only escalated as the high school years went by. He managed to avoid arrest, didn't impregnate any of his girlfriends, and graduated by the skin of his teeth. Three days after graduating, he joined the army.

Mrs. D'Angelo felt relieved at first. For the first time in eighteen years, she would not have to wonder what Rusty was doing and with whom. She did enjoy her other boys and take pride in their accomplishments, but she never stopped missing Rusty. He came home once for Christmas, and once for a week on leave, but other than that, Rusty was gone.

He'd send a postcard occasionally, but he rarely called and didn't seem to be interested in how his family was faring without him. She told people who asked about him that he was "finding himself" out in the big, wide world, and one of these days he'd come home to his roots. She prayed that this was true, and after twelve long years, her prayer was answered.

She picked up the ringing phone before leaving for her secretarial job at the Catholic elementary school and sat down hard on a kitchen chair when she realized it was Rusty calling.

"Ma, it's me, Russ. I'm in Massachusetts. I'm on my way to see you."

"You're in Massachusetts?"

"I'm at a rest area on the Pike in Springfield. I should be there in about an hour."

"An hour? Good Lord, I was just leaving for work."

"I guess I could look up Manny and Diego and come see you later," he offered.

"No, no. You come straight here. I'll work things out. Do you remember how to get here?"

"Have you moved?"

"No, we're right where you left us."

"Some things you never forget, Ma. I'll see you in an hour."

"You drive safe," she said, before the line disconnected.

She put a hand on her heart and willed it to beat more slowly. Her son was coming home to see his mama. She didn't really know where he'd been for the last decade or why he stayed away so long, but it didn't matter. All that mattered was that he would arrive soon, and she could see him and put her arms around him.

She called the principal of the elementary school and told her she had a family emergency and wouldn't be in. In the eleven years she'd worked at the school, this was the first time she'd called out. They'd just have to do without her today.

Mrs. D'Angelo fixed her hair again, fluffing up the dark parts to cover the gray. She put on some lipstick, changed into her nicest blouse, and then picked up the phone to call her husband. No, she thought as she put it down again, this is my time. I want to see Rusty alone.

She sat in a rocking chair and closed her eyes, thanking God for finally answering a mother's prayer. When fifty minutes had gone by, she opened the front door and looked out at the beautiful day. The sky was a cloudless blue and the sun felt warm on her face. After a few minutes a shiny, black BMW pulled up to the curb and a tall man with neatly combed black hair and a black mustache got out of the car. He wore jeans and a white polo shirt with a light gray sports jacket and had a bouquet of flowers in one hand.

Mrs. D'Angelo stood frozen, trying to reconcile the skinny, wild boy who'd left for the army twelve years ago with this good-looking, polished young man. She opened the door wider and squeaked out, "Rusty?"

Her son laughed and ran up the steps, wrapping his arms around her. "It's me, Ma. In the flesh."

She cried many tears that morning as she sat with Russ, as he now called himself. She fed him her homemade ricotta cake, showed him pictures of his brothers and nieces and nephews, and listened as he filled her in on his life. He'd learned computer science when he was in the army and when he left after six years, he got a job in a small technology company. He was now the boss, with ten employees who reported to him. He owned his own home, had a beautiful girlfriend he was engaged to, and when he told her the worth of his company, she shook her head in amazement.

"Why did you stay away for so long?" she asked.

"I wanted to make something of myself. I wanted you and Dad to be proud of me."

"But twelve years? That's a long time."

Russ was silent for a moment before speaking sadly. "I didn't make great choices for the first few years after I left the army. I was drinking too much and had a hard time sticking with one job. I was going nowhere when I got in an accident, which was like a bucket of cold water over my head. I finally woke up and decided to be the man you and Dad always wanted me to be."

She reached over and held his arm lightly.

"There's something I never told you Rusty, I mean, Russ. Something you should know." She told him about Sister Irene's prediction of how his life would turn out and how she had refused to believe it.

"Why didn't you ever tell me she said that?"

"I didn't want to put the idea in your head that you'd land in jail someday. I knew you were a good boy who liked to push the limits. But I never believed for a minute that there was anything bad about you. I believed in you. I've always been proud of you. You didn't have to wait until you were rich and successful to come home. You've always been welcome here."

Rusty cried, then hugged his mother and told her he loved her. Once they'd dried their tears, they called Mr. D'Angelo and Rusty's three older brothers. As soon as they were able, they came to their childhood home to welcome the wanderer. Mrs. D'Angelo made sure she took plenty of pictures—Russ in front of his shiny BMW, Russ with his arms around his brothers, Russ with his nieces and nephews on his lap, Russ smiling between his proud parents.

The next time she went to St. Columba Home for Religious Aged she brought a stack of printed photos of her family taken the day her bad boy came back home. She found Sister Irene, now very old, and showed them to her.

"Russell D'Angelo. I remember him well. It seems he turned out better than I thought he would," the old nun said.

"Do you remember telling me that you believed he'd end up in jail?"

"Hmm. I probably did. He was always in trouble if I recall."

"But I always knew he'd turn out fine, and he turned out more than fine."

"I thought I was the expert on children back then, but I could have learned something from you, Mrs. D'Angelo."

"And what would that be?"

"The sisters believed that discipline was the way to handle difficult children back then, but I think we were wrong. The way is love. And you are the embodiment of that love."

MY ROOTS
Mackenzie Scanlon

My roots wander, no matter how lost I am.
When I can't figure out who I want to be, my roots tell me
that I can.

Growing can be hard and confusing at times,
But it's crucial and needed, just like leaving the past
behind.

Some of my roots are exposed and above
the surface,
And I hope that I don't fall.
Even though my roots will forever be in
the ground,
I want to stand for a purpose,
Strong and tall.

NOT FORGOTTEN
Marilynn Carter

Ancestral roots run deep
Spreading from
  generation to generation

parents, grandparents, siblings,
     friends, lifetimes, worlds
offshoots wander thru
     time and place
As many, depart earth
     return
          in new form
photos reflect back
     stimulate memories
          stories swirl, tumble out
wondering and wandering
will we meet again

GOLDILOCKS GRANDMA
Michael Young

We can give to our children only two things,
One of them is roots and the other, wings.
–original author unknown

My wings have taken me to West Africa, Europe, and the Middle East, and to living in New England. But my roots are in the Yakima Valley of Central Washington State. Now, when I enter a pine forest and smell the evergreens or walk on the soft crunch of pine needles, I'm transported back to the woods of the Cascade Mountains with their majestic snow-capped peaks, their icy cold lakes, and streams of crystal snow runoff. I remember especially one vacation when the whole family packed up and headed for the hills. The temperature of The Valley was in the 90s to 100s, while the mountains were in the comfortable 70s. We even got Grandma and Grandpa off their farm for a while. Little did we know the adventure that awaited us.

Grandpa Herman was as tough as Grandma Ida was sweet. She was not a minute over five foot tall and he stood at six foot plus. Yet they were always a team, which is to say that they complemented one another. His light complexion was tanned and his hands rough and calloused. His eyes were like blue steel. A first-generation German farmer, his language was sprinkled with good ole Anglo-Saxon words. She was kind and gentle, a preacher's daughter with a passion for growing African violets. Grandma always sent me cards for birthdays and Valentine's Days signed "Your Old Flame."

They worked side by side on the farm, milking cows, picking asparagus, and planting a huge vegetable garden. It was hard to get them to take a vacation since they needed someone to tend to the animals and water the crops. Cows with full udders don't go on vacation, and chickens need to be fed, eggs collected. Yet in a farming community, neighbors would be good neighbors, and everybody stepped up and helped out. One summer in the 1950s my mom and dad and sister and I got together with Grandma and

Grandpa to go camping. Now Grandpa was fond of going to the Saturday farmer's auction to look at cattle. He'd often pick up something on the side, whether he and Grandma needed it or not. I suppose that's where he found the old army surplus walled tent that we lugged with us on our camping trip.

Up in the Cascade Mountains near Rimrock Lake, the Forestry Service had created campsites on old dirt roads. There was usually a place to park, a heavy rough-cut picnic table, a fire pit, and a tent site. And, most important of all, a heavy, galvanized trash can with a tight lid, chained to a tree because there were bears. It was at one of these sites we parked our cars and pitched our tent, which came with tent poles, guy ropes, and plenty of military-grade stakes. The tent material was a heavy, waxed, olive-drab canvas with a tent flap at the front that snapped and tied shut. The thing was big enough for all six family members and all our stuff. Sturdy enough to survive combat conditions, once it was set up and staked down it was not going anywhere.

While sister Susan and I played, the men set up the tent, and the women "made camp." A red and white checkered oilskin tablecloth was laid on the picnic table with plastic knives, forks and spoons, and paper plates. A kerosene lantern and citronella candles provided light for the night and relief from the mosquitoes. A Coleman stove was what we had to cook with, and a plastic basin was what we had to do the washing up. We had an insulated cooler with ice for refrigeration. That constituted our kitchen and dining area except for the "grub box," which contained our food for the weekend.

After supper, the plates were thrown into the garbage, and the pots and pans scrubbed. The grub was packed up and put into one of the cars except for some crackers and cookies placed in tins. Dad played "Pretty Redwing" on his harmonica while Mom tucked us kids into our sleeping bags. Shadows flickered from the fire and the Coleman lantern as the grownups chatted and caught up on news of other relatives. The smell of campfire and pine trees hung heavy in the still mountain air. The sound of a nearby stream soothed us with a lullaby, but it was not easy to fall asleep. We were not home in our own beds, plus there was something else.

Both Grandpa and Dad liked to tease and play practical jokes. But was it them or the black bears we had heard, shuffling, and snuffling around outside the tent? Susan and I comforted ourselves by saying that bears would probably not come around while the grownups were still awake, visiting by the fire. Besides, the noises were probably Grandpa, trying to scare us.

After we kids had fallen asleep, the lantern extinguished, and the fire put out, the grownups got to bed. It was with a start then that we were all awakened. From the picnic table, there came a clattering, a clanging, and a banging. It was the marauding bears! Food tins and pots and pans were being scattered everywhere.

Grandma was not about to have her camp picnic table trashed. We all sat up startled. In my bleary-eyed sleep, I saw Grandma momentarily in the tent door before she dashed out.

"Woof, Woof, Woof!" she barked at the bears as she rushed toward them, clad in her apricot-colored summer nighty.

With little hesitation, Grandpa stooped out the door and shouted, "Ida, what if the bear don't run?!"

I have never seen a little old lady move so quickly as when Grandma made a U-turn and sprinted back into the tent. The clattering stopped. When we decided that the bear had been frightened away by my mighty Grandma, we all went to sleep and slept the night. Next morning, we arose and inspected the carnage. The kitchen was reassembled, we kids had Kellogg's Cornflakes from the grub box with milk from the cooler, and grownups managed to salvage the percolator and retrieve the can of Folger's Coffee. After a satisfying breakfast, we went for a hike to walk it off.

While I don't remember if we stayed another night in that particular campground, I will never forget Grandma's battle cry, "Woof, Woof, Woof!" and Grandpa's admonition, "Ida, what if the bear don't run?!" I wonder if the bear will ever forget being chased by a grandmother in a pink, nylon teddy! I'm sure I won't.

This an excerpt from Michael Young's unpublished memoir.

MY MOTHER'S ROOTS

Quinley Sologaistoa

My mother's roots coil around me like vines
She is in my everyday
My every word
The ice on my tongue longing to sound like hers
For hers is strong and unbroken
But mine is quiet and timid
The words that flow from my pen itch to have her voice
For hers are strong and unbroken
But mine are quiet and timid
The gleam in my eyes ache to strike like hers
For hers are strong and unbroken
But mine are quiet and timid
Her strength will seep through those roots into mine
The ice will bite with her power
The words will flow unbroken
My eyes will strike unforgettable
I will be able to say
"I am my mother's daughter."

WAITING FOR MOTHER
Catherine H. Reed

Momma never knew her mother
or her name or what she looked like
One day while outside on the steps
the old lady next door came over,
looked at her and said, "I know your
Mother" and left. She did not see her
again, for days. One day she came over
she did not sit down. Put her finger to her
lips and whispered "your mother is an Indian
Princess. She is very pretty and has long,
brown hair. You look like your mother.
She's coming to get you on her pony and
take you home with her." Suddenly,
a woman next door came out yelled at the old
woman. "Get back in the house." The old woman
scurried away.

That night there were no more tears.
She got in bed with her hat, coat, and shoes on,
her doll in her arms and a bag with some clothes…waited.

UNFORCED ERRORS
William Belisle

"I'm not moving the couch," I say in response to yet another of her unrelenting requests.

"But I'm pretty sure I was sitting on the couch before." Mona counters.

I stand firm.

"There is no way in—" I stop myself. "There is no way your teeth are under that couch."

Like always, her reaction is either one of self-pity: "Nobody ever wants to help me," or the ever-popular passive-aggressive: "It's fine. I just won't be able to eat anything tonight."

Mona is my sister. She's four years older than me and visits like clockwork every Christmas.

Breathe, just breathe, I remind myself. After all, Mona is… what's a nice word for it? Eccentric?

Every year when Mona comes from Massachusetts to visit my wife and me in California, it always starts the same way: an email from Mona asking what dates would be best to come for Christmas. We'll reply with something like: "Mona, it'll be great to see you. Between the 22nd and the 27th works best for us." However, instead of coming for five days, Mona books her tickets for a nine-day stay. Apparently, Mona considers the dates we provide her as more of a suggestion than anything else.

"It's not worth flying across the country for only a few days. But don't worry, if that's a problem I can stay at a hotel," she replies, trying to sound like she's being flexible.

She knows with utter certainty, however, that she won't actually stay in a hotel. We'd never let her because that would mean having to pick her up and drop her off at her whim. And she's very whimsical. And oh yes, she doesn't drive.

"Mona," I say, "when was the last time you had your teeth in?"

"What?" she says with a quizzical expression, as though I had just stepped off an alien spaceship. She has no idea what I'm talking about.

"Your teeth, your false teeth, the ones we've been looking for. How could you lose them anyway?"

Mona loses something every time she visits: hearing aid, glasses, wallet, purse, watch, pill container, keys, coat. And today it's her teeth.

Last Christmas she arrived at the airport without her plane ticket. The agent said, "No problem, what's your name?" For reasons known only to Mona, she gave the agent her maiden name, which of course the airline had no record of. She ended up buying a new ticket.

When she arrived at our house, she told the story as if it was the airline's fault. "I've been using my maiden name since Frank died three years ago." Frank was Mona's husband. After he died, Mona just decided to use her maiden name, but without telling anyone or officially changing her name. In Mona's world, if she changes her name, everyone else just needs to catch up.

I had asked her how much the ticket cost, because a last-minute ticket close to Christmas must have been expensive. She proceeds to pull a mountain of papers and paraphernalia from her massively overfed purse, then can't find it. She doesn't remember how much she paid and doesn't want to talk about it anymore.

Mona would be a sure winner on *The Price is Right*. In her purse-a-palooza, there is a high likelihood that she has every bizarre item ever requested by Bob Barker since the show began in 1972.

Frank and Mona were kindred spirits. He found Mona's quirky habits to be charming and endearing. I would tell you about Frank, but, *de mortuis nil nisi bonum dicend um est* (of the dead nothing but good is to be said).

Mona is five feet two inches of crazy. Her wild and frizzy hair sits atop a thin wiry frame that has more energy than a Mentos tablet in a bottle of Diet Coke. Her dark eyes and somber expression belie her frenetic energy.

At our house, she's afraid that Alexa is listening to her every word and cups her hand beside her mouth to make sure it can't hear her.

She wraps ground coffee in a paper towel, secures it with a string, and orders hot water at restaurants so she can brew her own coffee at the table.

She spends excessive amounts of time on utterly confounding tasks, like picking out kidney beans one at a time from a pot of homemade chili to make a burrito for lunch. At dinner, she hunts through the garbage for empty cans or boxes to make sure the ingredients list doesn't contain words with more than three syllables (which would be very bad but she's not sure why).

Mona is red meat free, gluten free, GMO free, MSG free, and eats only organic food. Yet offer her a cookie or something sweet and she will fight you for it like it's the last pork chop on the boardinghouse table.

When Mona loses something, the more she thinks about it, the more convinced she becomes that what she's lost simply must be beneath, behind, or hidden by the heaviest object in the room.

One of the reasons Mona loses things is because she has an unfortunate tendency to wrap things in Kleenex. Once wrapped, she can't see them anymore and doesn't have to worry about them. Out of sight, out of her mind.

Once, she wrapped her hearing aids in Kleenex "to keep them safe." Later she was eating a bowl of nuts and, as near as we can tell, she wiped her face with the Kleenex, the hearing aids dropped into the bowl, and one was included in her next handful of nuts. The audiologist at Costco did an admirable job of keeping a straight face when we explained how the hearing aid had gotten crushed between Mona's teeth.

Looking for a lost item, Mona follows me around the house the way a dog will when you go to the kitchen for a snack; not necessarily because they want a snack too, but because, well, just because.

There's tension in the house which I feel behind my eyes. There's no chance it will be relieved until—or unless—the teeth are found. In the moment, I can't step back far enough to see the humor or the absurdity. I want to not care but I can't.

Suddenly I become aware that I'm smelling popcorn popping. Of corse! She has found her teeth but didn't think to tell me. I'm simultaneously relieved and annoyed.

She was sure she had checked the spot where the teeth were found and is now convinced that someone was playing wild mind games with her. I'm sure she thinks it was me.

Later in her visit, she asks a question that seems innocent enough. "Do you by any chance have any blue paint?"

"Maybe," I reply. "I might have some in the garage. What is it you want to paint?"

"I brought a mobile for the baby that I want to give it to her for Christmas, but it needs to be painted," she says.

Knowing that Mona has a rather casual relationship with cleanliness, especially with things that come in liquid form, I thought it would be best if I helped her. We still have an archipelago of diamond-hard super-glue on our countertop from the last Mona visit.

I find a can of blue paint and take it outside to the picnic table. Then I get a tarp to cover the table. And it's windy outside, so I place heavy rocks at each corner of the tarp.

I scrounge around some more and find a small paintbrush, a jar of water, an old rag, a screwdriver to open the paint can, and a paint stirrer. When everything is finally ready, I invite Mona outside to paint. With an expression of pity and a hint of indignation, she says: "The mobile's not ready yet; it needs to be assembled first."

Of course it needs to be assembled first. How had that not occurred to me?

I help her assemble the mobile, which means that I assemble it because she's lost the instructions.

Finally, everything is ready for Mona to paint. She goes out to the patio and takes one look at the paint and says: "that blue: it's too dark. I can't use that," then goes back into the house. She now has no interest in finishing the mobile, and I am left putting away the paint supplies. And the tarp. And the weights holding it down, and the paint stirrer. And whatever is left of my desire to help her.

Next day, she asks: "Can you take me to the store?"

"Umm, okay, what kind of store; what do you want to buy?"

"Well, back home, I belong to a drum circle, and I thought I'd buy supplies to make a drum."

Somehow, I had completely missed the fact that we'd need a drum on Christmas Eve.

"Where would you buy these supplies? I don't know where you would get something like that, especially on Christmas Eve."

"Oh," she replies "Any hardware store will have what I need."

At the hardware store she finds a plastic pail, a dowel to use as a drumstick, and a large pipe clamp to fasten the drumhead to the pail.

"Oh darn," I say. "I don't see anything that could be used for a drumhead. Dang."

"That's okay," she assures me. "I brought one with me!"

Just what I needed to hear. In the game of tennis, they talk about unforced errors, such as serving out of bounds and giving your opponent a point not because they earned it but because of a mental lapse on the part of the server. Mona lives her life committing unforced errors.

For better or worse, however, Mona is family. A few times I've even thought there's a good chance she was put on this earth as a test of my ability to handle stress. If that's the case, I'll have to live with it. Our parents died several years ago and Mona is all the immediate family I have left.

As we wade through this life we are given, I often think the most difficult thing to master as an adult is figuring out what's important and what's not important. For Mona, what's important is visiting her brother every year and making sure her grandniece has a gift to open.

For me, what's important is: it's Christmas, I have a grandchild, Mona is family, she's my sister, and I love her. Those are important. I just wish my back would stop hurting from moving that couch.

NEVERTHELESS, SHE PERSISTS
Laurie Rosen

"Storms make trees take deeper roots."
            —Dolly Parton

In North Hollow, a silver poplar blown
down by Irene, beckons from a meadow.
Her roots face the road, fanning outwards.
A waving hand—long fingers grasp
for light and carbon dioxide,
some still cling to earth,
sucking nutrients.

Every spring bare branches sprout
pearly buds. In summer, leaves shine green.
Cool fall turns them yellow, orange,
then brown—they scatter, a halo
around her head. Winter buries her
beneath white quilts, only her
uppermost twigs left exposed.

Always spring returns
to warm the frozen landscape, softens
the bed where she rests, coaxing her
to consciousness.
Altered yet unstoppable.
Awake and reborn—she rises.

Previously Published in *Sisyphus*, Fall 2018 and *The London Reader #MeToo: Stories of Survival*, Winter 2018

BENEATH THE BEYOND
Kathryn Chaisson

Lina stepped carefully over the thick crawling roots, avoiding the slippery green patches of moss covering the weathered bark. Pressing an age-spotted hand against the uneven surface for support, she searched along the oak tree trunk for the special object that she remembered from long ago.

Earlier that morning she found herself unable to focus on the book she was reading. Even the witty lines by her favorite author and an intentionally busy lifestyle couldn't keep her latest wave of sadness at bay. It didn't help that every little thing seemed to weigh on her spirit lately—an influx of bills, car problems and never-ending home repairs. Mostly, she was missing Will.

Over the years since his passing, she had learned how to navigate unexpected low-level grief triggers through creative distractions and meditation. This time around they didn't help.

From her reading spot on the window seat, Lina looked across the room at the row of framed family pictures aligned on a bookcase. Her eyes rested on the silly selfie Will had taken of the two of them camping. She smiled at the memory. They were a tight pair, always finding new adventures through the simple things in life. So many times she was eager to tell him her news of the day—how she loved her new volunteering project, her idea to redecorate the basement on the cheap, and which pro football team she randomly picked to support this season, only to be reminded in a flash of realization that he was gone. Time had slowed the landslide of grief that had often set her on the path of depression, and she had developed a strong determination to never go there again. She knew too that Will wouldn't want her to live that way.

Lina opened her book and struggled to stay focused, hovering over each word as though she were a beginning reader. Frustrated, she pointed her finger in the middle of a sentence to mark her place, tilted her head back and groaned loudly at the ceiling.

Something across the room caught her attention. On the wall behind the bookcase an arc appeared in graded colors like a rainbow. Surprised, Lina turned to the window to find the source of the colorful display which measured about four feet by two feet. The sun was shining in the room, but not at an angle that would produce a rainbow shape. There was a glass candy dish on the table, but the sunlight wasn't close enough to reach it. Instead, a misty sunbeam pierced through the grove of trees in the back yard near the oak tree as though it were guiding Lina to look in that direction. She spotted the colored glass wind chime hanging from the back deck and saw that it was projecting a tiny imprint of colors onto the white plastic lawn bench. She looked around for more rainbow type reflections and chuckled as she remembered the video of Will posing beneath a rainbow after a summer storm, pointing to it as though he were really within reach of it. Lina felt a sudden burst of energy, as though she had just awakened from a good night's sleep.

Still covering what she had yet to read, Lina lifted her finger, looked down at the word and froze. *Prism*. Thoughts came pouring out. Prism. Rainbow. Will. Tree…A memory began to form from her childhood, something that she had long forgotten. The time when she and Will first met.

Decades ago, she could see the oak tree from the same back porch with the dangling wind chime. After she and Will were married, they purchased the home from her parents and raised three children there. Her father once measured the distance from the porch to the wood's edge to be as he said, "about a half a football field away."

When their children moved out and started their own families, Lina and Will often took walks in the woods, starting at their property line and hiking to the abutting conservation land where Will had been a forest steward and nature guide. These woods were his second love, and to honor his wish, Lina buried his ashes at the base of the old oak.

Lina felt inspired to share her rainbow experience with someone and invited her neighbor Maryann over for lunch. The two lifelong friends laughed over the long-forgotten tales of their childhood shenanigans, reminiscing about the neighborhood games, their crushes, and Maryann mentioned what the kids called The Rainbow Tree, the nickname for the oak tree just beyond the grove's edge. Back then, a youngster with a scientific mind had the idea to hang a prism on the young oak guessing that with the right timing it would catch the sun's rays, creating a dancing spectacle of colors. It was also the day she met Will who was new to the neighborhood. It was Will who produced the idea for the prism.

In her pre-teen years, Lina watched the midday sun cast its bright, blinding rays into the budding woods where few trees had grown tall enough to provide adequate shade. Lina told Maryann about how the view of the tree line beyond the woods had become obscured by a forest of fully mature trees that allowed only a small amount of sunlight to poke through gaps between the canopy of branches and leaves. Maryann was pleased to hear that some wildflowers that they used to pick for their mothers still existed.

The midday sun peeked in and out from behind swiftly passing clouds. Lina reached the side of the tree where decades before the prism caught the sun's rays and awed the children with its rainbow display. Lina looked for the prism, but it wasn't where she remembered it to be. She searched the ground near the base of the tree, guessing that over time it could have fallen, or a strong wind had blown it away. She dismissed the thought that it could be gone forever and hoped instead that a curious woodland creature carried it off somewhere. Disappointed, she placed her hands against the tree, lowered her head, closed her eyes and frowned.

A crackling sound coming from the tree caught Lina's attention and she felt a small vibration pass through her hands. Instinctively she pulled back and examined her hands for signs of a misdirected bug. Checking her palms and fingers she found them spotted with a mud-colored substance. Thinking she had unintentionally placed her hands over tree sap, Lina carefully took a closer look. Stuck to her skin but causing no discomfort were pieces of bark. Puzzled, she removed the bark pieces, and as she did, another crackling sound drew her attention back to the tree. On the spot where she had moments earlier touched the bark, imprints of her hands had embedded in the tree.

Lina looked around the woods and toward her yard but found nothing out of the ordinary, nothing until she noticed the absolute stillness in the air, the absence of the usual outdoor sounds. No bird songs, cawing crows, rustling leaves, or chattering squirrels. With her heart pumping faster than usual, Lina's first instinct was to race home and lock the doors. She looked again at her handprints that had become part of the tree. Slowly and upwardly, she scanned the towering oak, which to her resembled a guardian soldier standing by for her protection. This tree would be impossible to climb, she thought, not like the pine trees she used to ascend when she was younger. Its massiveness suddenly made her feel small and vulnerable and she felt the urge to bolt out of the woods. As she was about to turn towards home, something glistening high above her reach caught her eye. Squinting to get a better look, her mouth dropped open in disbelief. Dangling from a frayed and weather worn leather shoelace hanging from a metal railroad spike was the prism. *The* prism.

Lina now understood why it was difficult to find. As the tree grew over the years, the prism rose with it. At that moment, the sun escaped the line of clouds and like an arrow shot a ray directly onto the prism, revealing a multi-colored display once again. Lina marveled at the once familiar sight and wondered how the prism had remained untarnished by New England weather after all those years. She saw the spike and on impulse apologized to The Rainbow Tree for any pain it might have endured when the spike was driven into it. A muffled sound like background chatter made Lina look around for approaching people, but she saw no one. Listening closely, she realized the sounds were coming from the exposed tree roots. The unison of sounds broke into individual soft whispers that mimicked human conversation. Instinctively, Lina placed her hands back over the bark handprints. A small burst of energy from the tree sent a warm liquid-like sensation surging through her hands and feet, connecting her with the flow and feeding of each wandering root like nerve endings connected to one life force—the Rainbow Tree—with Lina as the conduit.

A shimmering pocket of light appeared over the bark handprint. Muted colors and movement within the light sharpened into a series of images that Lina recognized as moments from her past from an onlooker's point of view that only one person could have witnessed—Will. Tears flowed down her cheeks as she and Will reviewed some of their moments together. Minutes later, Lina heard another crackling sound and the voices and vibrations suddenly stopped. She watched as the bark handprint reformed into a fresh new bark layer and Lina, like the tree, had become rejuvenated.

THE LARCH
Molly Chambers

Tall and strong you stand
Late sun rays light your trunk
Your fluffy green branches
Reach out in all directions
Like a ballerina's tutu floating
Green ivy climbs up your trunk
A gentle breeze lifts your skirts
It seems you could take flight
On the cool soft breeze

ULTIMO

Thomas Reed Willemain

A victim of locked-in syndrome, Will lay immobile. Eyes closed, drugged, only vaguely terrified, Will imagined the scene around him as he drifted.

Will had once seen a play in which an old guy gave a grand finale speech to a circle of weeping loved ones. That wasn't going to happen with Will; he'd figured that out a long time ago. He knew the odds were that drugs or pain or the aftereffects of some surgery almost always took away the big moment. Will took a little satisfaction in having been right about that. In any case, not starring in that ultimate scene didn't feel like too much of a loss. Here and there, and in little ways, he'd made it clear that he loved them all.

Will sensed that his son was sitting across from his bed, half asleep. Will surprised himself by thinking up a little phrase: *Half asleep with grief.* He thought it was a pretty good end to all his tortured attempts at wordsmithing. It had taken him years to stop mourning the death of his technical life, but it seemed to take only a few seconds to put down his imaginary pen. That seemed wrong, but so be it.

Farther out, Will could picture his daughter rushing to get the kids dressed, packed, and in the car. The girls were taking too long to decide who would get to be dressed like Elsa and who would have to be some other cartoon princess. But the real problem was their older brother. Nicky knew why they were making this sudden trip and didn't want to go. The last time he'd seen Grampa he'd gotten yelled at for acting up. Nicky didn't want to think about all this, and his nine-year-old brain couldn't think of any other way to cope. But he knew he'd have to go, he'd have to say goodbye, and the scariness of it all would haunt him. What little Nicky didn't know in that moment was that all of this would someday be the opening scene in his breakthrough film.

Even farther out, Will's younger sister Jeannie was checking airline schedules and discovering there was no "compassionate policy" unless the body was already cold. It was odd to think that she'd now be the oldest. Amid all her hustling, while she was trying to decide between two pairs of shoes, she suddenly remembered the small act of childish cruelty that had always bothered Will, even though Jeannie told him more than once that it was long forgotten. Will had taken her deep in the woods behind their house. He'd sat her down on a log at the edge of the swamp and told her all about Yeti, the Abominable Snowman. When he could see that she was good and spooked, he'd suddenly run off and left her alone and petrified. She would need to come up with a better memory to share when it was her turn to tell Will's story. Or, she thought, maybe Will's regret for that one cruel act *was* Will's story.

Will sensed his son leaning over his bed, squeezing his hand, saying something he could not make out. Will tried to squeeze back but could not move. Will's last conscious thought was that he'd just missed his last chance to show something not easily said.

Then Will was back in his beloved woods. He was young and lean and fast, and he was running, running, flowing around trees, leaping over obstacles, alive with speed and full of a joy he hadn't felt in so many years.

When he finally stopped running, he found himself again at the edge of the swamp. Another kid was sitting on the log, facing away, watching two birds high in the branches of a maple tree. As Will approached, he suddenly felt the deepest sense of peace. When the kid turned around and smiled, the '50s crew cut made him look a lot like Will, and nothing like his pictures in the stained-glass windows.

WHOSE WOODS THESE ARE, INDEED I KNOW
Laurie Rosen

I've walked the same loop for over three decades,
every incline, descent, creek crossing,

etched in my brain—
each bend and birch,

the stand alone red maple, clusters and patches
of sugar maples and lavender lupine,

the red house, blue house, a rambling white farmhouse,
its llamas, goats, cats and sheep.

In spring my eyes feast on fields of buttercups,
in summer, Queen Anne's Lace flourish

along the road, cows in every season
greet me in a familiar sort of way.

Still, I'm startled
by a pop of pussywillows,

a lenticular cloud that lingers over Mt. Killington,
how the trees have grown so high I can hardly see

Middlebury Snowbowl on the horizon,
and just the other day, in the molted woods,

where there never was before, a brook barrels
into a pool strewn with scarlet leaves.

When the lethal arrow punctures
my heart, as it so often does,

it's here I find the strength
to withdraw it

in one breath—
liberating tug.

Severed Roots

"SITTING DOWN TO REST"
KIMBERLY BECKHAM

SACRIFICE
Diane Hinckley

"So you found Hiram Boggs." Ms. Lilac Boggs wheezed out a laugh and nudged the pie plate closer to Sophia. The pie was earthy, tasting of the dirt cellar where the apples were stored. The kitchen window framed an apple tree, misshapen and skeletal against big-bellied November clouds.

"That's what we're hoping to confirm," said Sophia, "though the DNA test you took will tell the authorities what they need to know." An outstanding student, Sophia had been selected to interview the probable descendant of the skeletal remains found on an archaeological dig near the Quabbin Reservoir.

The discovery had horrified the professors. Native American remains could close the dig. Although many skeletons were carried off to museums in the past, without regard to the feelings of local indigenous people, now the law and public sentiment were on the Native Americans' side. But a Greek amulet found with the corpse had convinced Dr. Dorset, the dig's leader, that the skeleton was that of a Caucasian belonging to the modern era the students were meant to probe. The dig was pretty much an academic exercise, but it would provide a chance to check archaeological methods against historical records.

Sophia, having recognized the amulet as resembling one her grandmother wore, told her instructors she thought this person must have visited or even lived on the island of Crete. She'd wondered if she was looking at an immigrant from her own ancestral village—maybe someone who came here to work on the reservoir project—who somehow found himself murdered and secretly buried in Massachusetts.

The local newspaper had posted an article on the grim discovery, and Lilac Boggs responded with a letter to the editor saying she believed her missing great-grandfather was found at last. He was known to carry the amulet around in his dungaree pocket, and he disappeared shortly before the destruction of his hometown to make way for the Quabbin Reservoir. Now Sophia sat in Lilac's kitchen eating pie and answering questions, though she'd meant to be asking the questions herself.

"Did they find the stake?" Lilac asked.

Sophia's hostess, in her overstuffed flannel shirt and khaki pants, resembled a Halloween scarecrow filled with autumn detritus. The lady's hair was the color, and almost the texture, of pine needles.

"The stake?"

Lilac wheezed again, rocking back and forth. "I bet you were working with maps. You must know the skeleton was found at a crossroads. I suppose the stake rotted away. The old folks said it was ash wood."

Lilac's question explained the placement of some rotted wood between the ribs, as well as a hole in the ragged flannel shirt. Even so, Sophia was left speechless.

"They'd seen those crazy 1930s vampire movies. They got the idea of what to do in case of Dracula, but they didn't know what to do in case of Hiram Boggs." This was followed by another merry wheeze and a cough. "Or so I was told. But they figured that what worked for one kind of evil might work for another."

"They thought your great-grandfather was evil?"

"He wasn't always evil. Well, they said he wasn't. I never knew him. He was long gone by the time I was born. They said he picked up the *evil* when he was overseas."

"He was in a war? World War I?"

"No, it wasn't a war. It was a dig, like the one you were on, only it was on that island with the labyrinth and the Minotaur and all that stuff they scared us with in high school."

"Crete."

"No one should ever travel. I never have. I did visit a cousin in Toronto once, but I came right back. You have to stay with your roots, and mine are here, those that aren't under that blasted reservoir."

"Your family home was in one of the lost towns?"

"It was, but you're sitting in it. My family had it moved. They dug a dirt cellar like the one they had in Hiram's day. They even planted an apple seed from the old place. It grew into the tree out back, except apples don't breed true. They need to stay with their roots just like we do. I had to buy the apples I put in the pie at one of those you-pick-em places. The ones on that tree out back come out like wrinkled little stones. Ugliest things you ever saw. Only good for lobbing at coyotes that get too close to the house. The tree picked up some of Hiram's evil, maybe."

"How is it that Hiram went to Crete? Was he an adventurous young man?"

"He did odd jobs for some professor over in Amherst, and when the professor went off overseas in the summer, Hiram would caretake. Even going off to Amherst to caretake was an adventure for someone in our family, and his parents didn't think highly of it, not with plenty of jobs in the shoe factory."

Lilac jumped up and waved the coffee pot. Sophia declined another cup of gritty coffee.

"But one summer the professor took Hiram along to Greece on a dig. Hiram knew how to dig, I guess. He'd dug graves after school and in the summertime. One time he and his buddy dug into an old coffin by accident. Saw something they shouldn't. So, anyway, off he went to that Crete place. He came back different."

Sophia's family often journeyed to Crete to visit family. They came back sunburned.

"He wouldn't go to church. He started to say that all power was in the earth right under people's feet. He would talk, they said, almost like a minister about the roots in the earth and the worms and snakes that wove around the roots and the blind, furry things that burrowed past the roots. He said the problem with everyone in town was that they'd wandered away from the earth and the roots. He even said, and my grandmother never forgot this, 'The earth is a goddess.' They thought maybe he was drinking, but he wasn't known to drink."

Sophia thought of the amulet: the little ivory goddess with the golden snakes wrapped around her arms.

"Then the state came to wreck the town so they could fill the valley with drinking water for Boston. They pulled down the town hall. The people were sad, but they knew they were helpless. The story goes that Hiram looked at the devastation and shook. He said you had to treat the earth just so. He said that even digging a cellar hole should be like some kind of holy enterprise. He went off the deep end, but no one thought much of it at the time. They were all mad at the state. They figured Hiram was just saying what they felt. But then he started haranguing people coming out of church, telling them it was all their fault for rejecting the goddess. By now, they just figured he was crazy and never should have gone off traveling.

"Then the church burned. Not long after that, one of those engineers the state sent out was found dead on the ground with his clothes all ripped like from a bear's claws. But there weren't many bears around here in the 1930s like there are now. In those days, they shot a bear as soon as they saw one, and they hardly ever saw one. And the engineer had been seen at dances with a local girl, so people started to think in terms of murder, like maybe by a jealous boyfriend.

"Little Sally—oh, what was her last name, her family moved to Ware—got bit by a rattlesnake, and there weren't a whole lot of them around, even back then.

"The cows in Mr. Burnham's fields started to drop dead, probably from something they ate, but no one could ever figure out what it was. And all along, Hiram's running around telling everyone the earth is being violated and demanding a sacrifice.

"A lot of people laughed, while others felt sorry for my great-grandmother, who'd only married Hiram because she'd got jilted by the doctor's son. But some didn't laugh."

Lilac gazed out the window at the twisted apple tree. "Some started to listen."

"A sacrifice," echoed Sophia. "You don't mean, I mean, he didn't mean …"

Lilac smiled a strange, predatory smile. Sophia wondered if the lady was telling a tall tale at her expense.

"The doctor's son hated Hiram. I guess he was sorry about jilting my great-grandmother for that girl from Prescott, and being sorry made him mad, the way it does a lot of people. Anyway, just to shame Hiram, he was telling everybody as a joke that they needed a human sacrifice to save the town and the land. He'd grab girls and threaten to sacrifice them, and his buddies would laugh. Then it seemed like the whole town was in on the joke, but there's always some that don't get a joke."

Sophia kept quiet about what she thought of such a joke.

"Some," continued Lilac, "took it seriously and wrung their hands at the horror of anyone thinking such a thing, while others took it seriously and thought it might be worth a try."

A thump on the cellar door made Sophia jump in her seat. Lilac choked out another laugh as she got up to let a gray cat into the kitchen. "Good thing you didn't have that second cup of coffee. You're getting twitchy."

The cat hissed at Sophia. Lilac said, "Oh, you!" to the cat. "I like to let her down in the cellar to deal with the snakes. They slither in through the dirt walls. They'd turn my cellar into a snake pit if they had half a chance."

November dark now filled the kitchen window, and Lilac and Sophia sat under a cone of light from a fixture filled with dried-up insects.

"So, anyway, one day a couple of the fellows who were starting to take the whole thing seriously were out in the field with Hiram, and they'd got shovels, and they were digging a hole. The three of them were talking about who they were going to sacrifice from the town, and one of them said it should be an old person who'd die soon, anyway. Now, bear in mind, these are fellows who went on to lead respectable lives in surrounding towns. Everyone knew who they were and who their families were, back to the time of Daniel Shays and beyond. And they were helping Hiram dig this hole for a sacrificial victim.

"Hiram said, no, it had to be some young person with plenty of earning years ahead of him or her, to make it a worthy sacrifice, and he said one of these two fellows should volunteer." Lilac wheezed again. "I should've given up smoking long before I did. Let that be a lesson to you, young lady."

Sophia, who didn't smoke, said nothing.

"They didn't like what Hiram said, and they stomped off. Days went by, and a young man called Ted Hopkins didn't show up for work at the garage. The two fellows brought some friends back out to the field, and the hole was now all filled up. They dug, and there was poor Ted, all trussed up, and it looked like he was buried alive.

"Well, naturally everyone was horrified, but by now none of them trusted the state and the town was getting disincorporated. So instead of informing some authority, the locals took matters into their own hands. All those Saturday matinees at the movie theater showed them the way to go. The doctor's son was in charge, they said. He brought the stake. Three weeks later, he and my great-grandmother ran off to Arizona. They didn't believe in Hiram's talk about roots, I guess."

Lilac looked at Sophia with sly brown eyes.

"That field where Ted Hopkins was buried never did get drowned in the flood or covered with trees. That place still sits there all pretty, with wildflowers. Makes you wonder what would have happened if Hiram had made the sacrifice a little earlier in the process."

The cat stood yowling at the cellar door.

Sophia thought of the amulet in her purse. She'd been told to present the tiny figurine to Ms. Boggs, with the hope that Ms. Boggs would return it to the university's archaeology department for display. Now she hoped she could get out of this house and into her car before Ms. Boggs asked about it. She would take it back to the university and try once again to persuade her professors to return it to Crete. She put on her jacket and prepared to navigate the labyrinth of country roads in the dark.

THE NAME CASCADE
Ed Ahern

The same names percolate
Through a family like a roof leak.
And except for the Juniors and Seniors
no outsiders notice.

My mother's father was Edward Willman.
He had five daughters, so his name died.
Almost.

After what I suspect was an argument,
My first and middle names became
Edward Willman.

I have a cousin whose middle name
Is also Willman, without Edward.
Probably a compromise.

Family memory seems to die away
In three modern generations,
But I balked.

So our infant son was given
A middle name you'll guess.
A loving infliction.

Our son called when his son arrived.
And said the middle name was Willman.
The grandfathers are pleased.

HAUNTED RANSOM
Chele Pedersen Smith

Mireille.... Mireille....

My name blew through the curtains in celestial swirls. Gripping the covers, I slid further under the iris comforter, the one I picked from JCPenney's catalog as a sign of independence. Sid always insisted on bold stripes; he was too manly for flowers. But he'd left with his mistress a year ago so the bedroom was all mine. Too bad the purple quilt arrived looking more like blue denim, but at least it was soft. I didn't have the strength to return it.

Mireille... The whisper came again. Where was this coming from? How did it know me or how to pronounce my full name, Mere-ray? Everyone else called me Miri. Maybe it was a long-ago owner, prim and proper. After all, the house was originally Victorian before renovations in the '80s. Sid and I had bought it eight years ago when I was pregnant with Lucas, then baby Jaden arrived two years later. Yes, it must be an ancient owner. I'd track down deeds in the morning.

The whispers bothered me. Tonight wasn't the first time I heard them. They rose in cottony strings, pirouetting around whatever room I was in, but I could never see who it was. Out of nowhere while cleaning, or organizing pictures for my event photography business, I'd hear it. Whenever I washed the dishes or gave the kids a bath, the gurgling water sounded like ghostly hiccups.

I tried to roll over to sleep.

There's no use hiding from me, the voice hissed.

I bent the pillow over my ear. What the heck did it want? I was too chicken to get up and investigate, and I was definitely avoiding the dresser mirror across from me. I still had a trace of trauma from fourth grade—when my friends and I played *Bloody Mary* in the dark. It was creepy enough sounding like we were saying *my* name over and over. Still gives me the shivers. Anyway, there was one stormy night when something happened!

Concentrating on the shiny glass of the medicine cabinet, we recited the name three times, but we weren't sure who this Mary was or why we were summoning her. But it was the thing to do at sleepovers.

As we debated about the girl in question, lightning zapped the bathroom outlet behind us! Our eyes never left our reflection as we screamed and a spark flew out, creating an electrifying branch glowing white. My friends swore it was the hand of the *Virgin Mary* reaching out to us! Callie fainted, and Vera wet her pants.

Trembling from almost being electrocuted, I helped revive my friends. I tried convincing them it was just unfortunate timing. My friends insisted it was the mother of Jesus. But whatever we saw that night, we vowed to sit up straight in catechism from then on. The nuns were impressed. Vera took it further and joined a convent after high school.

Even though I was all grown up at forty, I wasn't taking a chance with a mirror.

Mireille… you're in my lair.

I swatted my hair before the actual word trickled down. This thing wasn't going away, and it had the nerve to think *I* was the intruder! Where was my skeptical self now?

It's probably no surprise these wafting sounds were louder at night, especially in the quiet of a ticking clock. I thought I was losing my mind!

One night, while reading *Harry Potter* to the boys, I was almost convinced it was a snake in the pipes. But that was ridiculous. I had a plumber check just in case. Nothing was found, of course, and it was more than I could afford, but I had to protect Lucas and Jaden.

Ha-ha-ha. Now in the bedroom, the whisper's laugh stretched over me, and I felt a presence pressing close.

Mireille Garey, you didn't try hard enough.

I awoke with swollen eyelids. Crap, I fell asleep crying again. Wouldn't you if an entity threatened your family's safety?

I ran a washcloth under cold water, but not long enough. I didn't want to hear a ghostly giggle. I pressed the rag over my eyes.

"Should keep the boys home today," I mumbled, but soon nixed the idea. It seemed more dangerous here than out there, and I had engagement photos to snap at noon. So I helped the kids get ready for school. Besides, this ghostly thing wanted me, not them, right?

After waving them onto the bus, I fueled up on coffee and turned my computer on in the dining room. I searched town hall records for the next hour. There were at least four different owners. One old chap, Julian August, was high on my suspect list.

Refilling my mug, I sighed at the disarray. A Cheerios box spilled over, while leftover oats floated in bowls of milk. I poured them out and reluctantly rinsed the cereal bowls. I heard something again. Water glugged in slow syllables, Gar-ee-eee. Gar-ee-ee … Your … name … should not be … hee, hee, hee.

My head was practically down the drain trying to decipher the message.

"Miri!"

The sharp voice made me jump and bump my head on the faucet. "Ow!"

"What are you doing? Drowning your sorrows isn't the way to go!"

"Oh, Vera! Thank goodness you're here." I turned off the faucet and dabbed my curls with a paper towel. I rushed in to hug my best friend from childhood. "And I'm so glad you're a real person."

She scowled. "Yes, nuns are still people." She smoothed her gown, straightening her habit.

"Oh, I know!" I assured. "I'm especially glad you wear the Holy cloth. I'll explain in a minute." I took another mug from the cabinet and poured us a round. "You're allowed to drink coffee, right?"

"Yes, in fact, that's why I'm here." She pulled a small bag of ground beans from her sleeve. "The monks near us started their own brand. Here, on the house. *Halo House,* that is. Now I'm thinking God sent me over for another reason. Thank goodness I got here in time."

"I wasn't offing myself." I squeezed the bag of beans and inhaled the roasted scent puffing from the vent. "Coffee Cloister.

Ha, that's cute and just what I need! Thank you so much." I squeezed Vera next.

We sat over steaming mugs at the kitchen table as I moved a pile of overdue bills onto the window sill.

Vera squeezed my hand. "Are you okay, Miri? I know Sid's exodus was a sudden heartache."

"I'm fine. Sure, it's been hard adjusting, but I wasn't trying to drown myself."

"So what were you doing, coloring your hair?"

Hmm, yes, let's stick with that. It's better than the real answer. But I couldn't lie to a nun, especially my best friend! After a gulp, I braved saying it. "Okay … I think this house is … possessed."

Vera leaned closer and put her hand on mine. "Miri, I am so sorry." She sipped her brew. "You've been having trouble juggling the mortgage and utilities, but I had no idea the bank took the house back! When do you need to leave? You and the boys can stay at the convent temporarily if you need to."

Mid-swallow, I almost choked, laughing. "No, not yet at least. I hope it doesn't come to that, but thank you for your generosity! I mean the house is actually possessed, like ghostly haunted! I've been hearing my name in breezes around the house and in the water! I was trying to listen when you came in."

"Oh! That's a relief; it's just ghosts." Then Vera shook her head. "What am I saying?"

"Great, you probably think I'm crazy."

"No, I would never. I'm not sure I believe in ghosts, except for the Trinity of course, but if you're being bothered by one, I believe you."

"Thanks. Do you think you can get a priest to come by? Or, hey, your idea about leaving is good! I should sell the house."

"Are you serious, Miri? Of course you are; you're the only one of us who ever was." Vera gulped back the rest of her cup.

Flipping open my eTablet, I brought up a website. "Calista Rome, Home Realty. Wow, looks so pro. Do you think Callie would handle the house for me? I'm two hours out of her jurisdiction."

"She would do anything for you. Same as me, especially after the way you handled *that* night and never told anyone the embarrassing results!" Then Vera laughed. "I'm glad we were at my house with necessities nearby."

"We'll always have each other's backs." I caressed the design on my tablet's cover. "So you'll get an exorcist?" I gave Vera my best puppy eyes. "Please? Selling could take a while, plus I wouldn't want ghosts bothering the next person."

Vera set her mug down with a clank. "We rid demons, not sure about ghosts. So it's only in the pipes or walls?"

"Yes, 'til last night, when I felt a heavy presence pressing against me."

"Oh, my!" Vera's lips twisted. She riffled the edges of her napkin. "Are you sure ... you know, that you didn't have a late date?"

"No!" I gasped. "I'm not seeing him ... anymore. Sid cancels a lot so the kids are home most weekends now."

I sprang up and arranged some ginger snaps on a plate, setting it between us.

Vera helped herself to a cookie. "What happened to Edgar? You thought he was so cute. Nerdy with glasses, but rugged somehow? I never knew those characteristics co-existed."

"Right?" I leaned close with a crunch. For a moment it was like we were teenagers dishing about crushes again. "Our free time didn't jive. It was temporary insanity. I shouldn't have messaged him in the first place, but when Sid hooked up with his high school sweetheart, Edgar popped into my head. He's an old flame. We had unfinished business, that's all."

Vera snapped her fingers. "That's it. The haunting entity must need to fulfill something."

"But what exactly would it want from *me* after all these centuries?"

"Just ask it."

"I-I'm too afraid. I don't think my voice would come out."

"You know the Bible says, "Ask and ye will find.""

"Vera," I tsked. "That's asking God or Jesus, not haunting spirits."

"Well, they *are* Holy spirits." She held her head high, her nose aimed at the chandelier over the table.

"You got me there." I snatched one more ginger snap and called Callie. She said she'd come over about four and do a walk-through.

The coffee klatsch was over in a blink. Vera had to hurry back, and I had to get ready for a photo shoot in Phillipston. In the shower, my thoughts clashed like cymbals. Edgar's firm abs popped into my head, but I forced them out and planned elegant engagement poses instead. I didn't like arriving without new ideas as backups.

Mireille ... Mireille ...

With hands caught mid-shampoo, my pulse froze. My mind had been too busy to fear the water. I felt foolish but with suds in my eyes, I squeaked out, "W-what do you want?"

Vera was right. I needed to confront this thing. To my surprise, the gurgle answered.

Ask again in reverse.

Frazzled, I arrived at Red Apple Farm and strategically arranged hay bales and pumpkins in front of a barn. On the drive over, my mind looped. Was the phantom a Magic 8 Ball? I wanted to shake it and get another answer.

I shone my light meter around to set the camera's exposure. Hey, wouldn't it be funny if it picked up a ghost? A burst of excitement rushed through me, eager to try this at home!

Checking my list on the wedding poses clipboard, I studied the betrothed couple's names, Jill and Jack. Well, ha, that would be easy to remember. The pair would arrive any minute, but I was antsy to get on with my ghost hunt. Hopefully, they were simple and cooperative. I didn't have the patience for a bridezilla today.

I heard giggles down the path. Good, right on time! I grabbed my camera, fully charged, and stepped out to meet the lucky lovebirds decked out in cowboy hats and western garb. Ah, so cute! They were sharing earbuds connected to an iPod.

"Hi, I'm Miri. Glad to meet you," I shouted. "Just relax and we'll have fun."

"Wonderful!" Jill yanked out their ear candy.

"Ow!" The man rubbed his ear.

Jill ignored him. "Mary, we want our wedding set list playing while we shoot. I just picked out the songs on the way over."

"Sure, but it's Miri with an *i*."

"Oh, sorry, Mari."

The fiancé took off his sunglasses and glared. "Miri?"

"Sid?" I choked. "What are you doing here?"

He knocked his hat rim back and squared his jaw. "Jill and I are engaged, duh!"

My mouth fell open and I began to shake. "You're *that* Jill? And since when are you Jack, and into the country scene?"

"I go by Jackson now. My middle name. New life, new wife. Not that it's any of your business."

A tight pang cramped my chest. He might as well have shot me with a dart gun.

"You're *that* Mari?" Jill snarked. She turned to Sid, hellfire flashing in her eyes. "You booked your evil ex as our photographer? I gave you one job."

"I didn't." He turned to me. "You changed your photography name!"

"I did not! It's been Pine Photography since before we met." Fighting tears, I trembled as I packed my camera. "You never pay attention. As usual!" I slung the bag over my shoulder and bumped past the devil couple as I headed toward the SUV.

"Hey, wait!" Jill called. "I want my deposit back!"

"No refunds!" I managed to zing.

I was still fuming when the boys came home. I invited my brother Leo to a video game fest with his nephews, and he showed up with pizza. Bless my brother!

Glad they were occupied and fed, I tidied the house for Callie's looksee. I spied the photography bag on my bed. My stomach clenched. Did I dare? With the lights off, I pulled down the blackout shades and shakily panned my room with the camera.

"Okay, Mister Ghostly, where are you?"

In the quiet darkness, the lens caught nothing. Then something glimmered. My heart quickened. Clicking the shutter continually, my pulse matched the cadence as two flashing eyes and a metallic smirk floated in front of me.

"W-what do you want?" I croaked out. I stepped forward, bumping into a rough, scaly form. I screamed!

Mireille Garey. Are you crazy?

Something grasped me, and then light flooded the room. Squinting, Callie's shape emerged, then Leo and the boys ran in.

Lucas grabbed my legs. "What's wrong, Mommy?"

"Nothing, sweetie. My friend surprised me. Now go beat your uncle at Mario Kart."

The boys raced Leo down the stairs.

"Callie, did you see it?" I gasped, "or at least hear it? It called me crazy!"

My friend crossed her arms. "That was me, you Looney Toon."

"What? Oh thank goodness!" I hugged her, then recognized the rough scratch of her wool blazer. When we separated, I noticed double brass buttons and her long, crescent diamond necklace, otherwise known as the floating face. I laughed so hard my side hurt.

"First, you're petrified and screaming, and now you're having a giggle fit. I hope you're seeing a doctor."

I scrolled through my digital camera. "No, I'm not dating anyone right now."

"That's not what I meant."

"I'm fine. See?" I showed her the glinting grin in the dark and we both cracked up. "There's really something haunting me, though. Can you put a positive spin on spirits in the listing?"

She surveyed the room, tapping on walls, pressing her ear against the hunter green sheetrock.

"I'm no expert, but it sounds calm to me." She stroked her chin. "I could say the house has lots of character."

"Yes!" I smiled, relieved. "So far it's just one but maybe it won't bother anyone else."

"Are you sure you want to sell? It's a big change, especially for the boys. Hey, did you always have that?"

Callie walked over to the dresser and caressed the scrolled embellishments.

My ears crimsoned. "Got it from the side of a road about four months ago. It was in great shape in a wealthy town far from here. I don't usually do that, but Sid took the chunky six-drawer dresser with him, and I was tired of keeping my clothes on the big chair."

"That's so selfish of him!" Callie seethed. "But I think you reaped a reward with this beauty."

"Yeah, I checked it for bugs and rats. Oh, speaking of which, you won't believe who my engagement couple was today!"

"Sid? No way! The gall. I bet they just wanted to rub their nuptials in your face. I'm so sorry you had to run into him." Callie rubbed my shoulder.

"What if it was a cry for help? Jill was mean and dismissive, even to him." I plunged back on the bed and sighed. "I actually felt bad for Sid. Maybe he wants to come back. Maybe that's why he accidentally booked the photos with me."

"No! Don't go down that path, Miri. They made hurtful choices, let them stew."

"But what if I didn't do enough to save the marriage? Maybe I should've been more ambitious, finished that Pilates class, or worn more makeup. Jill's a knockout."

"I'd like to knock her out!" Callie muttered. "You're doing better without him. Your business is blossoming, and so are you. Sid's a piece of work." She ran her hand over the dresser's ornate handles. "And so is this masterpiece. It's weathered but high quality and perhaps antique. How old do you think it is?"

"No idea. Should I sell it? Might cover some mortgage payments."

"Maybe, but it's an endearing piece. What if your ghost is coming from this? When did the haunting start?"

Chills prickled my arms. "About the same time!"

That did it. I threw clothes out of the drawers. Stuck in the back of one was a tarnished photograph of a man on a bicycle with a ginormous front wheel. "Strange. Was that called a penny feather?"

Callie took the picture and flipped it over. "Close. It says, *J on his penny farthing.*"

I was really creeped out now. "J as in Julian, previous owner of this house?"

What were the odds? We emptied the drawers lickety-split, called Leo upstairs, and the three of us lugged the empty dresser to the garage. But that night, the pesky poltergeist still taunted me, so they helped move it back the next day.

Callie put the house on the market and Vera snuck in Brother Benny from the Abbey to cast out the entity. He waved rosary beads, Holy water, prayers, and burning sage over me and every room of the house, including the running shower. In return, I paid him back by buying homemade coffee and jams from their monastery gift shop.

The first night I had the most refreshing sleep! Benny was a lifesaver, along with God, of course. In the morning while washing dishes, my mind drifted to wedding photo arrangements and the plumbing gurgled out *Gar-rey … Gurrrl … Loser.*

"Maybe you have a clown in your septic tank," Callie joked on the phone.

"I hate that movie. Can you conjure up a buyer pronto? I don't want to stay here another night. I'll even rent it out. Whatever's quicker."

"You're in luck. I have a showing today. I'll really push it," Callie promised.

And she did! The buyers were Jill and Sid, I mean Jack. Turns out, he never took his name off the mortgage so they moved in right away. At that point I didn't care. In fact, it was kind of funny. Let them be haunted now. I leased a townhouse in the school district.

My brother, Leo, borrowed a U-Haul, and his buddies helped transfer the furniture. As the kids and I settled into our new place, I felt free, financially, too.

"I bet the demonic duo was behind the ghosting all along!" Callie declared on closing day.

"Yeah! Well, the joke's on him now."

We broke into champagne and toasted my new sanity.

Pirouetting to my room, I flopped into bed and lounged in the dark. Ahh. I snuggled into the covers and shut my eyes.

Mireille …. Mireille.

What the hell? I bolted straight up. "Jules, I don't have your bicycle!"

It should have been you ... Mireille ...

I bent the pillow over my ears, vowing to call Callie in the morning.

"He followed me, Cal! How do I get out of my rental agreement? I need another place."

"What? How? Moving is a pain," my realtor friend reasoned. "Give it another night. Maybe it's just a habit in your head."

"Habit! You're a genius. Vera said we could stay with her if need be. What better way to test it out."

Over the weekend, we bunked at the convent. The boys had a blast. There was a big birthday bash at the orphanage nearby, and I snapped photos to earn my keep. It was the most serene sleep we ever had. The thinking pattern was broken!

Sunday night, we looked forward to our own beds. I clicked off the lamp, snuggled under the covers and drifted off to slumber.

Mireille ... Mireille

"Oh no, not again! What now?"

Hurray for Mireille. Your name is a beautiful bouquet.

I sat up, suspicious. "Now you're complimenting me? *Why?*"

Did Julian want to date me?

Mireille ... You really make my day.

Wow, the thinking pattern *had* changed. "What gives?"

You take my pain away. I've never heard your name before.

"What B.S.," I grouched. "You've been hissing it for months!" But then I stopped. Something about it sounded familiar.

The ghost and I recited the last line together. "Until your heart walked through my door." Ah, it was the first love note Sid gave me. I switched on the lamp.

"Why would a ghost know?"

I scrambled to the window. Was my ex serenading outside? Under the streetlamp, I didn't see anything nor hear a peep. Running through the apartment, the only ones there were the kids fast asleep.

I paced my bedroom. On the fourth circle around, it hit me. Of course! I hurried to the bed, throwing sheets aside. How could I forget? I loved Sid and that first note so much, I saved all of his sappy scribbles. When we married and moved into our first apartment so bare, I cut a slit into the mattress and stuffed them inside, along with a copy of my favorite wedding photo.

Fumbling for scissors in the nightstand, I clipped the stitches. Fishing the notes free, I fanned them out and cried, re-reading each one. The past months made sense now. I hadn't fully grieved the split. Then I gasped. The divorce finalized the day I found the dresser! I had driven home aimlessly from the courthouse, my mind in a fog, just like my heart and confidence had floundered, feeling lost this past year.

It was the love notes that needed burning, not sage. What haunted me all this time was a bed of lies. In the morning, I dragged the mattress to the curb and went shopping for a new one.

DUSK IN SUMMER
Bradley A. Michalsson

The cicadas are humming,
an insectile frequency that layers
the landscape, filters the world through
a gauze of white noise.
All is effervescence.
The twilight is tinted by the murmurs
of countless creatures heralding the coming night.
Blossoms from the arthritic apple lay,
discarded swaddling clothes, mottling
the tawny field with pink pointillism.
The sun dips and reposes behind hills
offering themselves as a welcome shoulder.

I sit, a carpet of greenery as support,
part of everything and removed
from it all–a traveler on a train,
the landscape flashing by in frantic frames.
Never fully experiencing,
never able to capture each moment–
a firefly flitting through cupped hands.
Here in this expanse as the light fades–
so foreign, yet everything smells as home should:
glad breezes, soil, the sharp scent of growth,
and the pungent bite of trampled grass.

Can I follow where the light goes?

Not a question, a feeling,
a sense of connection, and its loss.
A final glance before departure.
It is sad, almost, watching the day end.
Light leaks weakly through a sieve of branches.
Beside me, the heavy stalks pray to the earth
and the earth sings back, a haunting
lullaby of slumber, of goodbyes.

THE HANGING APPLE
David Story Allen

Sprinkling the ashes of a deceased person is not unlike farting in a Goodwill store; it feels good, but no one really notices any change in matters when you do it. Richard shook the dust into Lake Mattawa, having twenty minutes earlier offered some heartfelt and pithy remembrances of his father, Edgar Lang. He thinned his lips and strolled back to the reception hall. At fifty three, he felt a bit young to lose his remaining parent, but there's no road map to such journeys. His sister always thought that their father would have died in some raid the day before he was to retire from the FBI, but he made it out of the Bureau alive. Sepsis did what the New England mob could not, although he felt painted with shame when the Bureau's collusion with Whitey Bulger came out.

Back in the hall, guests commended Richard on his eulogy. Cousin Fred from Belchertown nodded from a corner and raised a glass to him. His slurred small talk suggested that it wasn't his first, but Richard wasn't in a judgmental mood

"Well … guess he atoned …Your dad did."

"Atoned?" Richard pulled a face. "What are you talking about?"

"Maybe not. The FBI and all … In Boston anyway …"

Richard folded his arms over his chest like a teacher awaiting a simple answer. His stern gaze and gray pinstripes had no effect in producing anything from Fred. Later by the buffet table, Richard asked his father's former partner what the cousin might have meant by *atone*.

"Hard to say." A booze-burned Brian Dennehy-type thinned his lips. "I recall that guy —the cousin—from your dad's retirement party. Seemed he never met a Manhattan he didn't like. I wouldn't give it too much thought. But that reminds me. I've got something in the car for you."

Richard made a lunch out of the bacon-wrapped scallops, and in less than two minutes, his father's partner returned with a file.

"Your dad left this at the Bureau years ago. Some nice commendations in there. He might notta talked about them all.

Anyway, yours and your sisters' now." Another thin-lipped smile, a pat on the shoulder, and he was gone.

Richard lingered as the crowd thinned, thanking everyone and not wanting to turn the page on this last chapter in his father's life. When it seemed that only the people working at the reception were left, he got to his Volvo wagon, but did not start the engine. The lot was pretty empty, which was a bit of a metaphor, it seemed, for the rest of his day. Looking at the manila folder on the passenger seat, he pulled the pincers off and began sifting through the three inches of documents which spanned as many decades. Papers were in no particular order: a letter signed by Hoover about good work intercepting drugs in Vermont, a photo that looked like his father was testifying at a hearing in D.C., a wanted poster for Joe "The Animal" Barboza, and a clipping from *The Boston Globe* that included a mention of his father tracking the route of the hijackers to Boston for 9/11. At the very back was Edgar's original paperwork to join the Bureau in 1976. The application included addresses that Richard had heard of, including some from the days before zip codes. A line on page six caught, then riveted his eye.

Father: Harvey Lang. Deceased 1975.

Richard squinted at it to be sure that he had seen it right. He loosened his tie, and cast a glare of puzzlement at the paper. He placed the yellowed page six on top of the folder and started the car.

Winding up Route 202, he had no desire for music. His face gave the impression that he had just smelled something unpleasant. Normally, such cloudless September afternoons would make for a pleasant drive toward Orange, then north after Route 2, but that line on page six had its hook in him. Given his father's age at passing, there was a limit as to where he could go for answers, but as he neared the state line, one came to mind.

Not at the service was a great aunt in Fitzwilliam, New Hampshire, whose recent hip replacement had kept her from the service. A few summers ago, Richard had painted a front porch for her, so he felt fine dropping in unannounced.

The yellow clapboards on the rambling Victorian probably had issues beyond paint, but Richard wasn't about to start making suggestions. To people of a certain age, his great aunt reminded people of the "Where's the beef?" lady from the old Wendy's commercials. She smiled while opening the Dutch door, asked about the memorial service, was not surprised at who wasn't there, and produced a plate of cookies that had probably passed their sell-by date. After a few minutes of small talk, Richard moved his Queen Anne chair a bit closer on the threadbare Oriental rug and took a deep breath before asking,

"I was always told that my grandfather disappeared during World War II. That's what was always said. Is that correct?

His great aunt held his gaze and gently put her coffee mug on top of a *Yankee* magazine that had hosted more than a few of them.

"I … never saw him after the war. But, my mind's not what it once was."

"But," Richard countered, "I never met him, and I found something that—"

"I was in Michigan in those days," she broke in. "My father was at a converted car plant that made B-17s. I didn't see your father after our childhood until I was back east. Years later."

"Okay, but …" Out of his suit jacket he pulled page six. "This says Harvey Lang—I know that was his name—died in 1975."

He waited for a response but she was like stone, but he detected just a slight steeling of her eyes. "I was born in 1970, and I never met him."

He sat back and crossed his legs. "Am I missing something?"

After a long ten seconds, she looked away, then back to speak. "I didn't have much to do with the folks back east, as I said. I was in Michigan. We didn't come east until, well … Reagan was president. During World War II, people … died. They went missing. They went off to … They settled elsewhere … Sometimes they went where the work was."

"Hmmm …" Richard's face looked like he had just been told his car needed new brakes. "Okay, but, a death in 1975. In the family? Does *that* ring a bell?

She exhaled and forced a disingenuous chuckle. "At my age, y'know, I've been to a lot of funerals. I read the obituaries to keep up with my friends!"

It was clear that either through age, the scarcity of details to life before the internet, or something else, that this was going nowhere. He tucked page six back into his jacket pocket.

"Still watching *Jeopardy! after dinner?*" he asked.

She was, but wasn't thrilled over the new hosts. Pulling out of her driveway, he thumped the steering wheel and swore.

Reaching Peterborough as the afternoon began to fail, out of nowhere, his brain's inbox clicked. His father's friend from boarding school was in an assisted living community in town. Before the Bureau, before the service, and before Dartmouth, Edgar was at Mount Hermon School – now Northfield Mount Hermon – in western Massachusetts. Whenever Edgar visited Richard, he looked in on his roommate from those days. Before reaching the center of town, Richard turned down a tree-lined street and then up the circular driveway. Recalling the fellow's name at the desk, he was directed down some hallways smelling of urine. He came to a room where an octogenarian who reminded him of some president recognized him from an earlier visit with his father. The news of Edgar's passing eventually forced a thin smile of resignation. "It happens at this age … Quite a life, your dad's."

Richard asked him if he recalled anything about his grandfather while they were at Mount Hermon in the 1950s.

"Never met him," came the response. The tone wasn't taciturn, but matter of fact, in a Vermont farmer sort of way.

"Do you remember him ever picking my dad up at school for vacations? At graduation?"

"Can't say I do. Any reason you ask?"

Richard explained, and his father's roommate pursed his lips.

"I think you'd be more interested in your dad, especially how he just left us, more than, say, his father."

Richard explained that as a government document stated Harvey to have lived until he, Richard, was five years old, it baffled him that he'd never met him.

"Hmmm …" the Biden look-alike nodded. "Well, that's going back a bit. Your dad was a good man though. He was who I knew."

Richard thanked him, and said he'd be back to chat about his father sometime.

"I'd like that. Bring a copy of the obituary if you can."

Heading to his car, the word rang in his head. If Harvey Lang was dead, there'd be an obituary. After a couple of seconds, he rolled his eyes. "God-*dammit!*" There'd be no online obituary for someone who died long before there was an *online*. Home ten minutes later, he poured himself a darker than usual bourbon, and thought about contacting his father's school to see if there were any records of who to contact in case of emergency and the like. Given the years, it was a longshot, but boarding schools love to keep records.

Halfway through typing in the school's name, on a whim he typed in Harvey Lang. Nothing. Then, as if a bell in another part of the house was ringing, it occurred to him that through ancestry.com his wife had established an account with newspapers.com. She was in California presenting a paper on Parkinson's, so he had to search the documents on their laptop for the login information. He got in and proceeded to tap his grandfather's name into searches for every decade up to his father's birth during the war. Fearing another dead end, he emptied his glass and typed in the last decade:1940 to 1950 – and there it was.

A 1975 issue of the *Manchester Leader*, a predecessor of the *Union Leader* reported that the execution by hanging of Harvey Lang was carried out in the state prison in Concord shortly after midnight on the previous, airless July night. Richard's eyes darkened and he glared at the screen. Scrolling down, he learned that Edgar's father had been convicted of bludgeoning a seventeen year old girl to death with a tire iron early one morning in 1969 at Weirs Beach in Laconia. The motive was thought to be an unrequited advance, and the evidence was overwhelming.

Richard sat there for a while, eventually searching for more information on the matter, then made a decision. If ever there was a time for an even darker bourbon, this was it, but he had to drive, and it was getting dark. Printing out several articles of the day regarding Harvey Lang and still in his suit and tie, he headed back to Fitzwilliam. His great aunt was surprised but not unhappy to see him again.

Come back to help me with *"Jeopardy!?"* Back in his Queen Anne chair, he handed over the pages from newspapers.com which explained why he never met his grandfather. His great aunt thinned her lips, looked skyward, then rested her chin on a palm.

"Why did you keep going at this?"

"Too many people told me to stop."

She muted the TV and tapped the arm of her chair. "It wasn't anything you needed to know."

"I don't *need* to know the prices in the Market Basket circular that I get weekly, but it doesn't hurt that I do. *Why* did this never come out?" He wasn't shouting, but he was neither simply curious nor patient.

"Oh, it was out! Believe me. Years later your father told me about his dad's antics when he, your dad, was in junior high. He never knew what he was about, Harvey. Your dad worried that his father's record – he had one even then – well ... it might have kept him out of Mount Hermon or Dartmouth or even the service. And having a father who's a murderer. He was sure the Bureau wouldn't take him in the 1970s after the trial. But they did."

"Why? I mean, why'd he ... *He* couldn't do anything about it."

"No, but you know how people are. Family roots. Same blood. Maybe a bad seed."

"So why couldn't he tell *me?* Did he think *I* was going to blame him for ... I don't know, any of it? *Really?*"

"He didn't know *what* you'd think. But I can guess. He almost did, a few years back. Remember that discussion a few Thanksgivings ago about slavery. Someone was talking about Faneuil Hall and how its name should be changed. When we were doing dishes, he mentioned that you seemed to think that the name of that building ought to be changed because of what that guy did. Faneuil I mean, although I don't remember the details. Your dad had quite a memory. That's why he was so good at the Bureau. I'm guessing he figured that if you thought there was some shame in a building in Boston being named for some guy with slaves, you might feel ... I don't know... " For a long time, it seemed that the only noise to be heard was the ticking of the Stennis clock on the sideboard. "*Jeopardy!*" had begun on the TV, but Richard was only half–trying to provide questions to the muted answers.

"Well," he sighed. "He was right, in one respect. I actually don't know how I feel."

His great aunt nodded a bit, and clicked the TV off. "Take a suggestion from an old woman, or don't. *Don't* feel bad about it."

"Don't?" Richard pulled a face.

"That's right. *Don't.* This … matter … It happened long before you were born. Your dad was in Vietnam at the time. As I recall, it involved some liquor, the girl was Asian … That war … " She waved a hand as if to wipe away the memory. Nothing you can do about it now."

"But this was my grandfather …" Richard's palms were turned upward, pleading.

"Who you never met. Don't go carrying this around. Don't be like these people in, where was it, California I think. I can't remember the details, but it doesn't seem to make much sense punishing living people, or making them pay for the sins of dead people. So you know, now. Nothing you can do. Or undo. Why punish yourself?" From her lap, she held up her hands in resignation.

Silently, the commercial ended, and it was now time for Double Jeopardy, when the scores can really change. Richard leaned over to give his great aunt a hug and wished her luck with her responses to the show. Outside, there was just enough light for him to examine the porch under his feet. On the top step, some of the paint he'd applied a few summers ago was peeling. Perhaps he'd return to touch it up in the spring. On his windshield, he noticed a few drops. He hoped that it wasn't raining wherever the Red Sox were playing that night. His father used to listen on the radio, and listening to them play might take him out of himself. He backed out of the driveway and headed home but never bothered to turn on the game.

WITHOUT EVEN SEEING
Mackenzie Scanlon

When I was brought into this world as a seed,
My roots started to wander through the depths of my being.
I was delicate and fragile,
But my roots supported me without even seeing.

When I moved out,
My roots wandered with me to a place that I called home,
I was finally anchored and I absorbed a life,
That only I could ever know.

At the end of my life, when I am old and gray,
I'll be buried in the ground next to the roots that made me.
At this point I will be dead,
But my legacy will last since my roots will forever be in the
ground,

Supporting me without even seeing.

THE ROOT CANAL
Kathy Chencharik

I awoke with a toothache and knew a trip to my dentist was in order. I was lucky they could fit me in on such short notice but they did. I never liked going to the dentist. When I was young and had a toothache, the dentist would always pull it. Nowadays, they try to save your teeth. As much as I disliked dentists, I have to admit, I do like this one. We both enjoy being outside. I enjoy kayaking and he likes to run. He recently ran in the Boston Marathon. I was impressed.

As I sat in the waiting room, eventually my name was called. I followed the dental assistant into a room, hung up my purse and took a seat in the chair. Soon the dentist came in.

"How are you today?" he asked.

"I'm fine, but my tooth isn't so good."

"Open wide and let's have a look."

"Okay, but first I saw a picture of you at the Boston Marathon near the front desk. Are you still running?"

He nodded. "I'll be going to Japan soon."

"Don't you think you should take a plane or a boat?" I asked, before opening my mouth, not sure if he got my little joke or not. I thought I caught a glimpse of a smile as he shook his head. "Do you think I'll need a root canal?" I added before I finally shut up and opened wide.

He looked into my mouth and said, "I think I see the problem, but we'll take a few X-rays."

He left the room while his assistant took X-rays. When he returned, he looked at the X-rays and then at me. "Are you still kayaking?" he asked.

"Yes."

"You said something a little while ago which reminded me of a waterway I meant to tell you about, but forgot."

"Really? Where is it?"

"Tell you what. I'm going to write you a prescription for antibiotics. It will ease the pain. And I'll write down the directions for you. I think you'll like it."

"Thanks, Doc."

"No problem. I'll want to see you back here in two weeks to see how things are going."

Two weeks later, pain-free, I returned to see my dentist.

"Open wide," he said once again. "Ah, just as I thought, only a minor gum infection. So, did you find the waterway? Were my directions okay?"

"Yes, thanks Doc. The directions were spot on. The Root Canal was the best place I ever put my kayak in, and it brought me to the most beautiful lake I've ever seen."

BENEATH THE BRAMBLE

Jessica Dawson

Shadows of night dance wildly about a thicket in the wood.
Beneath a thorny bramble—the darkest demons brood.
Evil-sharpened nails tip the gnarly claws that scratch
The black earth with twisting maps of evil plans to hatch.
While walking through that very wood, upon their den I blundered.
My mind in blinding torment—loss and tragedies unnumbered.
But what direction do I go to escape their forest maze?
Unable then to turn around or find passage through the haze.
The moon shone brightly back at me through unearthly eyes of green.
Though brilliant were the stars that night, my course, to me unseen.

Longing for the answers that could justify the rain
Of miseries, misfortunes, and unrelenting pain,
I dropped the veil around my heart then traveled to that wood,
For otherwise, I feared that place, as any mortal should.
Wandering the ancient forest with so many trails to take,
The bravest souls wouldn't dare—with sanity at stake.
The devils haunt this bramble, sniffing out the broken spirit.
Shattered lives go to those woods, not knowing they should fear it.

The demons know this very well and greet each traveler first,
Presenting them their options, always knowing which one's the worst.
Snidely grinning creatures part the ticket from below,
Revealing all the carven maps; the traveler's way to go.
Each traveler must choose one path, all others lead to death.
For that poor passerby– demons feed off sorrowful breath.
There is no sanctuary from the decisions one must make:
It's the very soul of the wanderer the demons long to take.

It was my turn to decipher my map beneath the thicket.
The answer to my questions—my personal pathway's ticket.
Knowing all the while I might never leave this hellscape.
I spilled my soul upon the ground to help the map take shape.

There was nothing left behind for me, just the road ahead—
And the absolution that I sought or my body lying dead.

Emptiness within my chest, the hollow sound of regret.
From the devils' map, I chose left, though my destiny was preset.
With one foot before the other, demons cackling right behind,
I blindly hoped the path I'd chosen had some peace for me to find.

POP

Janet Bowdan

Ever popped your back so loudly
it took your breath away?
Ever set to work to get the bittersweet
out of your mother's garden, pulled
thinking this weed was *not* going
to get the better of you, stupid root, until
the pop made you fall backwards,
your son calling *are you okay*?
As you crawl into the shade
your husband saying, *I told you*
not to pull and when
it is established that you are okay
your husband starts to explain
that *this* is how Larry Bird hurt his back
helping out on the farm and *this*
is why he would lie on the bench
to stretch his back during his final seasons
and everyone knew he was in pain
and he should have known better
than to work on the farm.
Someone has to do it, you think,
or the roots take over.

FINDING A WAY
Diane Kane

We were just twenty, and we thought we were immortal. But we weren't.

Debbie and I had been best friends since grammar school. We imagined the future, being in each other's weddings, doing things as couples, and our children playing together.

"When we are old and gray, we will still be friends," Debbie vowed.

"We will always help each other upstairs!" I laughed.

We believed we would stay connected like the roots of two trees that grow side by side.

One day, Debbie borrowed my car. She was supposed to come back later and pick me up. She didn't. She was alone; there were no witnesses. There was no one to say what happened, nothing to indicate why the car spun around on a corner and hit a telephone pole, clipping it off. She died instantly. And almost as quickly, I was lost. I wondered why it was her and not me. But what right did I have to feel sorry for myself?

Debbie's parents were devastated; her family was beside themselves with grief. There was no room for my sorrow. My loss did not compare to theirs. But to me, it was huge. I visited the cemetery alone after everyone had left. I talked to Debbie while staring at the granite stone with the date of her death—a date I wanted to forget. I touched the deep engraved numbers of her birthday, April 21. I wondered what happens to people's birthdays after they are gone. Is it just another day? To me, it was more.

I dreaded seeing Debbie's parents, Charlotte and Henry. I thought they would resent me for being alive while they had just laid their only child to eternal rest. I was so surprised when they welcomed me with open arms. There were tears, but there was so much love as well. I went to visit them every day. Soon, Henry went back to work, and Charlotte was alone. I would go during the day to sit with her. Then I realized the house was overwhelming with all its pictures and memories. So, I started to take her for rides.

Charlotte knew a lot about edible plants from her mother and grandmother. She taught me which mushrooms were safe to eat and which ones to avoid. I learned how delicious Fiddleheads are when sautéed in butter. Harvesting them in the spring when they are still tightly wound is best. We gathered wildflowers but left the lady slippers because they didn't take replanting.

Sometimes, we would get on an untraveled dirt road. I would get out and move rocks so we could continue our journey. The days passed into summer. We started to smile, and eventually, we laughed. A few times, we would come to an impassable road and have to turn around or even back up carefully. Those were the days we laughed the most. We felt Debbie was there with us.

When I introduced Henry and Charlotte to my boyfriend Tom, they loved him. Tom grew close to Debbie's parents. He would help Henry work on his car. We all took day trips together on the Mohawk Trail that Debbie loved so much.

Two years later, when Tom and I were planning to get married, we looked at the calendar and immediately knew the perfect date. We were married on Debbie's birthday, April 21.

The pain and the loss of someone you love with your whole heart never goes away, but there are special ways to pay tribute to their lives and keep them close in our thoughts. Every April 21, we say happy anniversary to each other and happy birthday to Debbie. It's much more than just another day. Our roots are still connected.

PREDETERMINED WANDERING WITH ROBERT FROST

Steven Michaels

How often have I tread this soil,
unsure of my path under these elms?
Frost said to take the other route,
but did he ever examine the roots
which would impede his path?
In his haste to hasten the miles
on no sleep
he would say:
cherish the moment.
Yet I stand immobile
at every crossroads,
fearful of tripping up on my trip.
Free will has yet to find me here.
In not choosing,
I fall victim to
whoever else's woods these are—
passively partaking in my predestination,
moving onward on a path
mirthlessly muttering
how the hell did I get here?
Awaiting the day when
the world ends
in either fire or ice,
fully regretting to seize the day,
desperately trying to go back
to mend my fences,
as I progress towards
my acquaintance with the night,
knowingly knowing: nothing gold can stay—
For none will be back this way,
lest it be under the soil,
resting peacefully free
and nourishing the roots
that others must watch out for.

WHISPERS
Eliza Murphy

Amongst trees
I hear them
whispering

Root to Root
we will stay
connected

Together
our forest
endures all.

THE EXAM:
DEFINE HOW YOUR ROOTS WANDER
Stacy Boone

Merriam-Webster is a reference resource. One purpose of a dictionary is to define a word's meaning. Sometimes, a great complexity results.

#

Instructions

This EXAM has <u>two</u> questions. Circle your best answer. It is conceivable that several responses are necessary to reach your final definition. Move forward as the instructions provide. At the bottom of the last page is space to write your final meaning in a systematic probe to define how your roots wander.

#

Question A – How might your **ROOT** be best described? Circle one.

- A considered foundation, like **BASIS** (continue to Numeral 1).
- The essential core, like **HEART** (continue to Numeral 2).
- A bond, like **TIE** (continue to Numeral 3).

#

1.	Circle the definition that most closely matches what **BASIS** means to you, then continue to Question B.

      a. It is something on which something else is established.

      b. An underlying condition.

      c. A fixed pattern.

2.	Circle the definition that most closely matches what **HEART** means to you.

      a. Something resembling a heart in shape (continue to Question B).

      b. Your emotional or moral nature (continue to Numeral 4).

3.	Circle the definition that most closely matches what **TIE** means to you.

      a. It forms a knot or bow (continue to Question B).

b. It functions to restrain from independence or freedom of action/choice (continue to Question B).

c. It might **CONNECT** in place or establish a relationship (continue to Numeral 5).

4.   Is your **HEART's** emotional or moral nature distinguishable from your intellectual nature?

        a. If no, circle emotional or moral nature and continue to Question B.

        b. If yes, circle how your intellectual nature is best defined.

            1. **COMPASSION** (continue to Numeral 6).

            2. **AFFECTION** (continue to Numeral 7).

            3. **LOVE** (continue to Numeral 8).

            4. **CENTER** (continue to Numeral 9).

5.   Circle the definition that most closely matches what **CONNECT** means to you, then continue to Question B.

        a. To join.

        b. To meet for transference.

        c. To establish a communication.

6.   Circle the definition that most closely matches what **COMPASSION** means to you, then continue to Question B.

        a. Sympathetic of others' distress with a desire to alleviate.

        b. The capacity to feel sorrow.

        c. The ability to feel another's unhappiness.

7.   Circle the definition that most closely matches what **AFFECTION** means to you.

        a. A moderate emotion (continue to Question B).

        b. A prevailing tendency, mood, or inclination (continue to Question B).

        c. A tender attachment like **FONDNESS** (continue to Numeral 10).

8.   Circle the definition that most closely matches what **LOVE** means to you.

        a. It is a strong affection for another arising out of kinship or personal ties (continue to Question B)

       b. It is the object of attachment, devotion or admiration (continue to Question B).

       c. It is an affection based on **BENEVOLENCE** (continue to Numeral 11).

       d. It is what you hold dear, as in **CHERISH** (continue to Numeral 12).

9.   Circle the definition that most closely matches what **CENTER** means to you, then continue to Question B.

       a. A central focus or basis.

       b. A thing that is most important or pivotal.

       c. The source from which something originates.

       d. To cause to be concentrated, like **FOCUS**.

10.   Circle the definition that most closely matches what **FONDNESS** means to you.

       a. A tender affection (continue to Question B).

       b. An **APPETITE** (continue to Numeral 13).

11.   Circle the definition that most closely matches what **BENEVOLENT** means to you, then continue to Question B.

       a. An unselfish loyal concern for the good of another.

       b. An act of kindness.

       c. A disposition to do good.

12.   Circle the definition that most closely matches what **CHERISH** means to you.

       a. To feel or show affection for (continue to Question B).

       b. To keep or cultivate with care and affection, like **NURTURE** (continue to Numeral 14).

13.   Circle the definition that most closely matches what **APPETITE** means to you, then continue to Question B.

       a. An instinctive desire necessary to keep up organic life.

       b. An inherent craving.

14.   Circle the definition that most closely matches what **NURTURE** means to you, then continue to Question B.

       a. It is **UPBRINGING**, like early training.

       b. It is **EDUCATE**, as to provide with information.

       c. It is **FOSTER**, to promote the growth or development.

#

Question B – How might your action of **WANDER** be best described? Circle one.

- To go idly about, like **RAMBLE** (continue to Numeral 1).
- To follow a winding course, like **MEANDER** (continue to Numeral 2).
- To go astray, like **STRAY** (continue to Numeral 3).
- To move in a path, like **COURSE** (continue to Numeral 4).

#

1. Circle the definition that most closely matches what **RAMBLE** means to you, then continue to Answer Sheet.
    a. To move aimlessly from place to place.
    b. To explore idly.
2. Circle the definition that most closely matches what **MEANDER** means to you, then continue to Answer Sheet.
    a. The complexity of a **LABYRINTH's** intricate passageways.
    b. To follow a winding or intricate course.
3. Circle the definition that most closely matches what **STRAY** means to you, then continue to Answer Sheet.
    a. To move from a fixed or chosen route.
    b. To roam about without a fixed direction.
    c. To move without intentional effort.
4. Circle the definition that most closely matches what **COURSE** means to you, then continue to Answer Sheet.
    a. An accustomed procedure or normal action.
    b. A progression.
    c. To run or move swiftly through or over.

#

Answer Sheet

Find your final circled word or words asked under Question A and Question B and enter below to best define how your roots wander.

#

Question A
My type of **ROOT** is best defined as

_____.

Question B
My way to **WANDER** is best defined as

_____.

~end~

REALITY VULTURES

Thomas Anthony

Go young woman; go young man
go on your search. Is it life you seek?
Well, you have life, just look around.
Review your assumptions; they will
disappoint you, for you are wrong.
Now go and see everything.

While you are traveling, dig down;
find the root. Don't put the
stuff you find in the same place or
you will learn the meaning of
critical mass. Don't ignore stuff;
just keep it in view.

In massively over-dated Europe,
everything is for sale. Put in your bid;
with bad luck, you'll win.
I hear the search for the really real,
is perilous. You think
you've found it, every time,
but you content yourself with
never reaching it.

Is culture a chicken with
insider knowledge of the egg? Be
indiscriminate, it is your
birthright. Eat too much, tell
an oldie and laugh aloud. Sing
a bawdy song and learn enough
to understand what you don't know.

Carve books in your mind,
let an ant pass by your shoe in
complete safety. When you have
been away long enough, come to
me. I will explain it all, and you
will show me where I am wrong.

GILFEATHER TURNIPS
Elaine Reardon

A pantoum for Carl who shared his Gilfeather turnip seeds with his neighbors.

They bought the old farmstead
on Flower Hill Road,
cleared and planted the back meadow.
Now they could see north to green Vermont hills

On Flower Hill Road
he saved seeds
where they could see north to green Vermont hills.
Gilfeather turnips his favorite,

He shared Gilfeather seeds with neighbors,
said they were earthy and sweet.
Gilfeather turnips his favorite,
pulled after frost, saved in the root cellar,

buttery and fragrant right from the garden.
He planted in the cleared back meadow
to bring sweetness to winter.
They bought the old farmstead.

Wandering Roots

"ROOT MONSTER"
DIANE KANE

SCHEMES ALONG THE SCENIC ROUTE
Chele Pedersen Smith

Savoring a bowl of chocolate chip cookie dough ice cream, have you ever wanted to excavate those little bits and see if they would bake? Well, in 2004, I finally gave into the nudge and, yep, they actually turned into tiny, crisp cookies! My kids and I marveled at the silly success and gobbled them in one gulp, feeling like giants.

Thinking outside the box, the words, "I wonder" have followed me my whole life. When I was seven, I tried baking a pan of brownies inside our upright stereo console while Mom napped. Since I couldn't use the oven, I always noticed how hot the cabinet got while spinning records, so logically, it could cook chocolate batter!

My half-baked ideas have taken me down offshoot avenues I may never have stumbled upon. In the early '70s, the stereo brownies failed, but around the same age, my imagination took flight. Since we lived above a store near a busy Connecticut street, we weren't allowed out much, for safety's sake, but there was a small grassy patch behind the three-family apartment house and the one next door. One winter day, I had a fool-proof plan that would have us making snow angels in no time.

"Let's throw our toys outside," I coaxed my younger brother, John. "Then Mom will make us go get them."

So, "Whee!" the playthings went flying from the second story window. It was brilliant and would have been triumphant—if Mom hadn't caught on and fetched them herself!

Creativity blooms out of boredom, desire, limitations, and other ways. We didn't know it then, but we were on welfare and barely scraping by, so it's a good thing my imagination churned out free entertainment. Around this time, I made up characters for me and John to act out. I gave the girls names I found fancy or exotic. Karen, a superior girl, had things I wished I had, like a pair of white sandals. She clomped around the apartment with a square block stuck to her bare heels. Then there were Big Cat and Little Cat Hernandez, brothers I think, and a girl named Denise, who was nice.

In the middle of my first grade schoolwork, I'd often stop and stare into space. My fluffy writing brain probably began percolating then, but I don't remember what drifted my attention away. Mom had to meet with my teacher because of this daydreaming dilemma. Maybe my stare off into space meant I was thinking how best to solve my worksheets. Maybe I was wondering when my artist-musician-hippie dad was coming back from a gig. Perhaps ideas were hatching for more characters to play with, or I was craving those white sandals I so wanted. (Shortly after, Dad surprised me with a pair, just in time for a field trip!)

After my parents divorced, Mom married a Navy fella, and our "alter ego playmates" moved to Hawaii, and then California with us, but they faded away by the time we hit Florida in 1976. That's when I began writing my Sherri Whitman mystery booklets in junior high, which I still have in a drawer! Besides, with characters now existing on paper, we probably didn't need our imaginary personas anymore since we had freedom to conquer the big outdoors.

I was our activities director and John pedaled along for the ride. We explored Navy housing and peered in windows of an eerie, abandoned officer's club. I was convinced there was a mystery going on. We returned to show real friends and hid a cassette player nearby to record evidence. When we played it back, we were sure we heard alien sounds! (Naturally, the experience was incorporated into a Sherri story.)

Another day, John and I went dumpster diving in a paper goods receptacle, collecting cardboard and scraps to build a small puppet theater to entertain our little brother. We amazed ourselves with how cool the drawstring curtain came out.

I can't imagine surviving the lulls in life without off-the-wall inspirations. As a little kid, we had early bedtimes. Being tucked in at 7 pm, especially in the summer light, made it difficult to fall asleep. One evening, I saw an object down the hall. The more I squinted and tried to figure out what it was, the more a shape appeared, and the more my mind was convinced it was a real mouse in a toy car! I even tried calling it.

"Here, Mousie, Mousie." But it wouldn't zoom toward me. Finally, I got up and inspected it up close. Turns out it was just a sneaker.

Early on, my imagination kept me delusional and entertained, and still does in my late fifties. (Mulling over story plots in my head has made MRIs bearable.) No wonder I became a writer in sixth grade! My fictional characters were constant companions in the midst of change and moving to new places, and I'm thankful they still are. I have a slew of new ones as my writing wanders and branches out.

Creativity has committed crazy ideas and perceptions. If you've read my eclectic Goodreads blog or any of my books, you're probably not surprised. One way to enjoy life is looking at the world through wonky lenses. And I don't just mean my favorite purple eyeglasses I can't read a thing without!

My abstract mind also sees animation in mundane objects. Random hearts, crosses, and funny faces pop up out of nowhere. Do you see them too?

I'm amused by the expressions made by tail lights on cars and faucet handles on sinks, and once in the grocery store while selecting potatoes, I realized one resembled a cartoon character with bugged "eyes" on each side and an indented half-smile.

One night, I poured honey into my tea and before I stirred it, the foam mingled, creating a stylish woman with long white hair. She was winking. Another time, it resembled a cute spirit.

And at the risk of receiving an invitation to the funny farm, one night, from a certain angle, my bathmat shag was brushed in such a way that I saw Jesus with his long hair and facial fuzz. He seemed to be holding a cup and saucer and staring at it in surprise. Perhaps he saw a ghost in his teacup too.

HAIKU: WEED
Allan Fournier

Not so bad looking.
Persistent. Your own style. But...
Why must you grow *there*?

HUMAN PLANTS
Allan Fournier

We are like plants, our roots sinking and searching into the soils of our childhood and later lives for sustenance and growth. Some of our roots are straight and true. Others get deflected by rocks and other obstacles, the frustrations and disappointments of our existence, which mold us into fuller, more resilient, more interesting individuals.

Many of us then uproot to live with another plant; e.g., get married. We share a new soil, a new environment, but we carry with us the elements and minerals of our upbringing. This "uprooting" is a more drastic form of "wandering," which can result in a more drastic form of growth and joy.

WANDERING ROUTES
Allan Fournier

My wife, my daughter, and I, residents of Massachusetts, had our invite to my wife's nephew's wedding in the Outer Banks of North Carolina. We had airline and hotel reservations. The wedding was still on, in spite of a recent hurricane. We flew into Raleigh-Durham Airport, rented a car, and drove to the hotel. Our room was on the second floor because the first floor had hurricane damage. It was dark. We got a good night's sleep.

The address on the wedding invitation suggested the venue was nearby, leaving us with time to kill, which we spent at the Wright Brothers National Memorial. From the Memorial, we drove straight for the address on the invitation. We found a building to the left of the wedding address, a building to the right of the wedding address, and in between was a vacant lot.

Now we were getting nervous. Perhaps we should have spent less time at the National Memorial. We hopped back into the car, found a nearby office, asked about the address, and were told it was a real estate number, something different from a normal street address, for Coldwell Banker. We called the couple's house from the office where we had sought information—this was the age before cell phones—but there was no answer. We continued our drive, now looking for a Coldwell Banker sign and the correct rental number, aka "real estate number." We found the rental house and stopped in, but there was no one there. Our nervousness started to feel more like panic.

Continuing on, we saw a sign for East Eckner Road. We knew the couple's house was on West Eckner Road, so we went looking. On the way, we saw a Coldwell Banker office and stopped in. It turned out, the people in the office were waiting for the wedding couple to check in. While there, we called the couple's house again, and, eureka, someone answered! The lady happened to be a wedding guest who happened to go to the couple's house to change her baby's diaper because the baby happened to, well, you know. The lady informed us that, since the realtor couldn't provide a one hundred percent guarantee that the first rental would be available because of hurricane damage (remember the hurricane?) the couple had rented a second property, but neglected to inform the first realtor and us. We got directions to the new house. The Coldwell Banker folks, understandably, asked us to ask the couple to contact them. We drove to the new house in time to attend the wedding reception, which was already in full swing. Thanks to a poopy diaper, at least we got to enjoy part of the celebration before hopping on a plane back home.

Epilogue: For years after that episode, my wife, my daughter, and I played a game: Be the first person to yell out "Coldwell Banker!" when spotting a Coldwell Banker sign on the side of the road. Extra point if the sign also had a picture of a dog on it. (Our daughter really liked dogs).

DO ALL ROOTS WANDER?

Barbara Vosburgh

Wandering roots can mean so many things. Most people think of their roots as the place they were born and raised. This can be a town, city, county, or maybe a state, but when they say you can never go back, they are right.

I went back to my hometown, and it has all changed. The drugstore with its rounded glass candy cabinet, lunch counter, and real cherry Coca-Cola is now a burrito shop. The area next to the Community Center where I would go and ice skate now holds a rather large gazebo. Knowing everyone in town is a thing of the past, and the street where I spent the first eight years of my life is now covered with grass. The house and street no longer exist. So I don't call that town my roots. I wandered away from it many years ago never to return to live.

My gardens are full of wandering roots. Did you ever try to pull up a clover only to discover it is attached to a very long stem with roots wandering throughout your entire lawn? How about those grass roots buried deep into the ground intertwining as they grow? My favorite wandering roots come from the plants given to me by friends and neighbors. The roots wandered from their gardens into mine to be carefully tended to.

A person can establish new roots by moving. After eight states and the Marshall Islands, I spent a lot of time establishing new roots. Not an easy task, but I am grateful to have experienced so much in my lifetime. Sometimes you bring a bit of your younger self with you. The first time I moved to Denver, I wrote to my mother, "MOM! THE GROCERY STORE DOESN'T HAVE MACINTOSH APPLES!" Truly a shocking experience for someone from Massachusetts. Mom sent a bag of macs to me. Every self-respecting Massachusetts pastry cook uses macs, right?

Then there is the root of the problem. First you have to have a problem and recognize it. Sure family and friends recognize your problem, but it has to be seen as a problem by the person having it. When I pointed out to my mother that she needed a hearing aid, her response was, "I do not! Lots of people can't hear!" So I called my brother to tell him mom needed a hearing aid and I needed his help to convince her. He decided Mom could make the decision on her own. Of course years later he got his own hearing aid and was glowing about it. Now my daughter is telling me I need a hearing aid. Obviously this is not a problem I recognize so there is no need to find a root for it. I tell her "I do not! Lots of people can't hear!"

My favorite is the root of all evil, and my oven is a prime example. I have been known as a great dessert maker for decades, but this oven in this house has decided I no longer will own the title. It's an old house with an oven that must have been manufactured in the sixteenth century. It either has an evil sense of humor or hates everything I put into it. It is the root of all evil when it comes to baking anything from cookies to roast beef. I get especially upset when my baking doesn't come out like it should. What are the wandering roots?" The root temperature wanders, I am sure, while I am baking. I really think I can hear the oven laughing at me.

Another wandering root is the "root cause." What is the root cause? Is it something in us or another person or a thing out of our control? A tree falls on a house. Is the root cause the tree or a person not identifying a rotting tree or a neighbor weakening the tree by poor trimming or gale force winds? A root cause may never be discovered and the reasons are wandering around the neighborhood.

Of course not all roots wander: square roots, tooth roots, word roots although there may be more than one, root beer, and root rakes with a good driver. Root houses can wander if they are built over a sinkhole or unlevel surface.

So I am taking all my roots and going to wander on. Go wander away now and root for your favorite team while I am gone.

SONG OF THE AIMLESS
Jon Bishop

One day, I left my home
To put down roots in air.
The ground is dry and dead,
So I said bye to all
Who would not ever flee.
Instead of being trapped,
I saw all kinds of life
In places far and near.
Unlike the rest of you,
I'm always on the move—
And move is what I'll do,
Until I someday die.

WANDERING ROOTS
Karen Traub

Wanderers can be human, plant or animal. Sometimes it is a calling that leads us to uproot from one place to another. Sometimes it's a force beyond our will.

As far as I know, for all of his twenty-two years on earth, Charlie Hamilton never left the state of Massachusetts. He was born in Shutesbury, moved to Springfield, died in Greenwich, was buried in Prescott, and years later, his remains were among the 7,600 moved to Quabbin Park Cemetery in Ware in preparation for the flooding of the Swift River Valley.

I grew up in Framingham, Massachusetts, graduated from McGill University in Montreal, Quebec, traveled through the United States, Europe and the Middle East, got married and moved to Shutesbury where I developed a passion for local history during my time volunteering as a library trustee. It was a visit in 2005 to the vault in the old town hall—holding in my hands the neatly handwritten minutes from the first town meeting in 1761—that had sparked my curiosity and led me to read town annual reports, hike the dirt roads and forests of my town, and conduct research in my spare time to learn the stories of the people who lived here before me.

Looking at his death certificate which I found on a genealogy website, I can't help but wonder why it was his mother, and not his wife, who was the informant who provided the details. That must have been hard for her. I knew from previous research that Carrie Powers Hamilton had lost her daughter Lucy, age six, to diabetes mellitus, twelve years earlier. Even with the birth, death, and marriage records available to me, I don't know much about the life of the Hamilton family. Charlie was no blood relation to me, and yet I can't help but wonder who he was, under what circumstances he left home, how he lived and what toll his death on August 20, 1904 took on his family. The death certificate lists the cause of death as "phthisis," which Google tells me is tuberculosis.

It didn't take much coaxing to get my friend Leslie to join me on a hike from Quabbin Gate 15 to the old Hamilton homestead in April of 2021. On a previous hike, we had guessed where the house might have been and noticed the deep green carpet of foliage that looked out of place among the wild ferns and weeds. I was pretty sure it was the same groundcover I had planted at my own home and wanted to return and see the flowers in bloom.

Now, on this warm, sunny spring day, Leslie and I make our way down the winding path, stopping to rest a moment as we always do, at the giant boulder covered in the leafy brown scales of liverwort. We cross the bridge over Atherton brook, marveling at the stone wall remains of the old mill. At the end of the road, we turn right and there it is: a sea of purple flowers that have grown and spread for a hundred years. I'm overwhelmed by the beauty and thoughts of a mother's grief. Oh myrtle, tell me the story of the people who lived here. Did Carrie plant in her garden a small patch to bloom in the spring and remind her of her children? What happened to the family when the water commission took ownership of the homes and removed all traces of life in the Swift River Valley?

Myrtle, also called vinca, or periwinkle, spreads underground by rhizomes which are stick-like roots that travel opportunistically in every direction. The plant also spreads above ground when the thin stems touch the earth and take root. Creeping Myrtle is thought to have traveled with people from East Asia, to Europe, and to North America in the 1700s. This vine-line trailing groundcover with glossy or variegated leaves grows vigorously, creating a thick mat and displacing native species.

All that's left of the life lived by the generations of the Hamilton family is myrtle as far as the eye can see; and my longing to know and share their story so they are not forgotten.

The myrtle didn't choose to come to this area. The people who lived in the Swift River Valley didn't choose to leave their homes. The Swift River Act of 1927 appropriated money to build a dam to create the Quabbin Reservoir. The towns of Dana, Enfield, Prescott and Greenwich were disincorporated, erased from existence. Along with the four towns, portions of twelve neighboring towns including Pelham, New Salem, and Shutesbury were cleared of human habitation for the reservoir and its watershed area. People who had lived here for generations were uprooted, cast like seeds on the wind as more than two thousand people were forced to become migrants and find a new home. Not only the living were displaced as seventy five hundred dead bodies were exhumed and replanted in other cemeteries.

Every sip of Boston's water contains a story of a family like the Hamiltons as the water flows 65 miles, 200 million gallons per day, originating in the hills from streams and brooks like Cobb, Briggs, Atherton, and Rocky Run, flowing down to the great reservoir that once was the west branch of the Swift River and east to quench the thirst of the people of Boston.

GROWING SEASON'S ALMOST DONE
William Doreski

After days of rain the earth
smells like a pulpit bible.
The plants you transplanted pray
for their souls. At first light they rise
to their knees and look around,
surprised to find themselves alive.

Today we should sport clean socks
and slurp coffee by the river.
That tough brown flux will prove
mightier than the government,
belching past the sandbags
strewn at the edge of the parking lot.

When we get home your transplants
will have decided to thrive although
growing season's almost done.
We've grown a little ourselves,
aging in place like junk cars
dumped in the woods. Refining

our aesthetic by scanning ads
in *The New Yorker*. Adjusting
our intellects by reading books
heavy enough to anchor yachts.
The transplants will sulk all winter
in tangles of whisker-white roots.

Then in April they'll recover
their senses and rise up singing.
Maybe we'll act out as well,
and the river, having forgotten
this flash flood morning, will greet
the new order with a smile.

FAMILY TREED
Ed Ahern

Too much knowledge can be upsetting.
Family records and lore tell me that I'm
half Irish, quartered English and Swedish.
To affirm provenance, I DNA tested.
The initial finding verified my beliefs,
but then they refined the results.
Much less Irish, English and Swedish
and big hunks of Welsh and Norwegian.
Who the hell were they?
And whose windows did they sneak through?

HIKING'S SECRET MESSAGES
Les Clark

At my advanced age, should I ever suggest to my knees: hey guys, let's go for a hike, you know, like the ones we trekked about long ago in the White Mountains, the less rigorous Monadnock and the gentler path up Big Blue in Milton, MA...why, the patella would panic. The tibia would tremble. And the femur...well, you get the idea.

***

I started hiking back in my Boy Scout days. I was also distracted by girls, so achieving merit badges took enormous testosterone effort. I lasted long enough to be awarded Camping (for my latrine prowess) and Aviation (since I was in the Civil Air Patrol and knew what ailerons did). My scout master loved the Blue Hills, but our walks started on the unyielding sidewalks of Blue Hill Avenue. Two miles on concrete to Mattapan Square (a Boston neighborhood) got us blisters and odd looks. Two more miles up the twists and turns of the Blue Hills Parkway led us to picnic tables where we gobbled PBJs by the jar and loaf. Our cerebral conversations involved girls, model planes, and why girls didn't like model planes. My dilemma lasted until I met my wife who believed hiking belonged in documentaries.

***

At seventeen plus, the Air Force introduced me to their version of hiking. We didn't spend much time admiring the scenery and the physiology of Texas creepie-crawlies. Ill-fitting brogans led to bloody socks (later celebrated by Curt Schilling) and the wailings of city boys. Ego-smashing admonitions by our DDIs (Demonic Drill Instructors) led to close encounters with high decibel screams, so we hobbled along, singing *their* song...side by side. Eleven weeks of Basic instilled endurance. Who knew a five mile hike with full pack would be a breeze?

I would find endurance later in 24-hour shifts as an Air Force installer at bases and outposts around the world—but that's another story. Oh here's one. At a base in Turkey, we had to hike to the chow hall passing tree-born bugs making the Texas ones look like mosquitoes. Hut! Hut!

***

After marrying, we had a son, and four years later, a daughter. While she didn't want to go (hid under her bed behind dolls and dust bunnies), my ten year-old son thought a hike in New Hampshire's Monadnock region would be fun, along with his friends and *their* dads. This bonding experience created far too much synergy and energy. Oddly-shaped walking sticks, admonishes of shiny leaves of three, throwable rocks, and whizzes behind wide trees were a hoot. I told my boy not to run. The trail was rife with roots just waiting to snare (and gobble, a la *The Wizard of Oz*) the careless and those who wouldn't listen. On the way down, my boy thought he'd dash ahead of us.

"Slow down," I yelled but he tripped. While he didn't break anything, he wound up with some interesting, prize-winning, purple boo-boos. I rose to his level of exciting things to do. We took to white water rafting and he to Pop Warner Football (his sister was his cheerleader).

***

I had many friends who wanted to explore Mount Washington. One such like-minded person I'd met at a credit union convention at the...get ready...Mount Washington Hotel, wanted the experience. Now this is a mountain whose dangers hikers should *never* underestimate. Make that never, never. If it's warm at the base at the start of the Jewell Trail, it could be snowing 6,300 feet up at the observatory. We made reservations for an overnight stay at the observatory with their advertised hearty supper and sumptuous breakfast. While it took hours to get from Greater Boston to the Kancamagus Highway, a late morning hike of four plus hours would still get us to the top in time for dinner.

We started at noontime, blue-sky sunlight. An hour in, we quickly donned waterproof ponchos because of a cool mist. Hours later, we somehow turned off the trail and got lost in the rain. I turned to my companion who I knew was not easily ruffled. "We're lost," I admitted. My friend invoked an epithet involving the famous English detective. I was asked, "Do you want to turn back?"

Like Popeye yanking out a can of spinach to best Bluto, I reached into my pack, retrieving my Presidential Range trail guide. It was pouring. We joined ponchos to see where we *thought* we were. We spied a dotted line primitive trail on my folded map. Serendipity prevailed. A few steps away, a washed out sign provided the longer, winding way to the top. By the time we checked in, more than five hours after we started, we eased open the cabin door with our elbows because our fingers weren't working.

"Good thing you remembered that map."

"Not to worry," I replied with some bravado, "I had a compass as well."

After a full breakfast the next morning, we started down in short sleeves, fresh clean air, and warm sunlight. Such are the moods of Mount Washington that's claimed many lives. Make that many, many.

***

Several years later I was with a new family and by default, a gaggle of lazy Pong and Pac-Man players whose eyes glazed over out beyond a foot. As lovely spring days enveloped New England, I thought, well, let me put those pathetically soft feet to work since their only exercise was sprinting to the school bus and shuffling to the dinner table.

On a Friday afternoon whilst they examined and questioned the supper meal contents, I announced, "We're hiking Monadnock tomorrow."

"Like, where's that?" the eldest asked.

"Like, Yugoslavia."

"Like, no, really?"

"Like true." I can play their game. I hate that word, by the way.

"Can, like (and they named a friend) come?"

I would find out later that misery did like, no, love company.

We set out early the next morning—breakfast on me. It's always on me. I used the Vulcan mind-meld on them to stock up on protein and carbs. I didn't want to hear the 'wah, wah, we're hungry' refrain. I checked again; the Monadnock round trip is rated short: 3-4 hours. The White Dot trail was, in the morning, easy and cool going up. On my advice, before we left, I advised them to take bug spray. Does anyone listen to an Air Force veteran who suffered through Jurassic monsters in the Texas and Turkish boonies?

Never ask the question to which one knows the answer. Bug repellant? Oh... NO! However, their spongy cerebellums had registered the need for sweaters which they wrapped around their waists. The youngest carried their water bottles. (Hint: Never be the youngest.) The Seven Dwarfs were never this enthusiastic. Hi-ho my keester. Little chipmunks covered their tiny furry ears with all the free and loose teen and pre-teen chitter chatter. United Nations interpreters would shut off their mikes. However, that fa-la-la went south once the mountain got warm. As we made it back to the road, out came swarms of black flies. The girls were screaming. They whipped off their sweaters and swung them like helicopter blades hoping to swat a few. Mais non! We ran (I think it was *their* first time ever) back to the safety of the car.

Like no one spoke to me for days, too busy applying calamine lotion.

***

On my final Mount Washington climb, I learned the most valuable lesson from another friend. He and I had climbed different trails twice before. Now, unusually serious, he looked at me and said, "We're heading up Tuckerman's Ravine." Valley is a G-rated word. Ravine conjures up sticks and stones will, well, you know and not to mention, serious rethinking, and I told him so.

"Oh, you'll be fine," he assured me. I wasn't.

It was the worst. The terrific weather was disarming. At some point the easy woodland incline suddenly turned...vertical. Okay, I exaggerate. Halfway up, I looked back at Dave who had positioned himself in case I lost both my physical and mental grip. To be honest, this trail is photogenic only if one is sitting at the bottom in a comfy chair with an adult beverage. But whilst grasping at the edges of rocks and hoping my sneakers didn't slip off a supporting boulder, I may have complained this was becoming impossible for my skills.

"Look ahead, Les. Look at the trail."

I steadied my position and dared do what he suggested. A peristaltic line of hunched over thrill-seekers jerked and jived ahead of me. My sweat was a waterfall, coating the smooth boulders born when the earth was new. Okay, so I'm a writer embellishing the past. Let's just say this trek was arduous. The rocks, soil, and roots curved gently away several feet ahead. I

219

moved slowly forward. As I did, more of the afternoon sky revealed itself. With more confidence, my pace went from caterpillar to caterpillar after coffee.

"See, Les!" the smart ass smugly said. "Always look over the horizon. The path will always disclose itself to you."

As I stood at the top of the bowl of Tuckerman's Ravine, which derring-do skiers hyperventilate over in the winter, I thought it best not to tell Dave his wisdom sounded like the writings of a fortune cookie. Although I've since lost contact with my friend, I carry and employ his words whenever the going gets tough.

If you refrain from running unprepared, life will present you with a workaround.

I learned that on the trail.

HIKING TO THE LOOKOUT TOWER, QUABBIN
Janet Bowdan

We wanted to bike with friends the day before
until the skies opened up and dumped sheets
of rain. Instead Noah and Blair murdered me
in a game of Hearts, after I'd spent the morning
putting tomatoes in the garden for future pasta sauce.
Tempers were simmering and the friends planned a hike,
especially determined for proper social distancing,
much to the distress of all the children: Noah
not liking hikes, the friends' son trying to maintain
a careful 6' distance, even if it meant
crashing into the poison ivy trailside, and their daughter
who had her roller skates on and needed road, road without
cars, rollerskating UP the steep hill to the lookout
while we adults hiked fast on the trail through ferns and pines.
Blair demanded that I check the book
because he thought we must have missed the turn.
We'd been hiking 40 minutes; it was only supposed to take 30.
Perhaps Blair'd read it wrong and the loop
was not an hour's hike altogether but an hour each way.
We sped past the ladyslippers with Blair calling back over
his shoulder: "they only bloom once a year!"
I'd already stopped to take a photo of them, then off
we go again to get to the Lookout where the daughter
says rollerskating up is the hardest thing she's ever done
and we all sit at least 6' apart for our picnic.

THE PARTY
Elaine Reardon

It was a virtual birthday party. The group of friends had gathered each September to celebrate their mutual Libra birthdays. They'd go out, have drinks, dinner, and enjoy an almost carefree night off from responsibility.

This year was different. Anna was turning fifty, the first of them to make the half century mark. She and her husband Conner had separated, with him going off on a vacation tour of Croatia, and her to deal with the repercussions and the angst of their teenage children. And while he'd been prancing about off the coast of Croatia, the borders began closing, one by one, because of COVID.

She'd held on to half-time work. She heard from Connor once: a guilt postcard. She finally sorted through what he left. His out-of-season clothes were all packed in bags in the attic. She tossed out his favorite stupid biscuits, old socks, and thrice-read paperback novels.

Anna replaced his battered book case with a sleek table with shelves underneath, from Ikea. She put a tray on the top, and had her bottle of wine with a couple glasses at the ready. When COVID cocooning ended, she'd imagined herself pouring drinks from this new perch, feeling like quite the new woman when that time arrived.

Thus far, she'd made a couple pots of jasmine tea when her daughter Maura visited once a week. Maura had just settled into her first apartment with her best friend, and would come home once a week. Anna tried to put on a good face for the first few months, but Maura wasn't fooled. Mom was devastated. Dad? Well, he'd better not show his face. The bastard! Off in Bolivia, it turned out, with a woman, not Croatia at all!

And so the group of birthday friends, together since school, wanted to be together, for this journey into the fifties, amid all the confusion of self-containment. They planned well. Everyone had a good bottle of something they had hung onto for a special event. They'd have a virtual party on Zoom. They all opened bottles, kept enough for themselves to drink, and delivered the bottle with its remains (at least 2/3 full) to Anna's front door. She had a special bin set out for deliveries. Anna ended up with several bottles of wine, one of whiskey, a cognac, and some homemade vodka.

On the night of the virtual party, Anna set up her bar with all her new bottles and washed her best glasses. The glass gleamed in the candlelight. They all dressed for the occasion, despite it feeling so informal through Zoom. Anna decided on a Spanish theme and made tapas. She sautéed padron' peppers, sliced chorizo, and set out olives. Then she set up small plates for her friends, almost like an offering at the altar. Her friends rooted her, and they still grew and celebrated together.

TREE PEOPLE
William Doreski

Christmas, strange tracks in the snow.
You think a Yeti is prowling,
but I suspect a hybrid
of the Ovidian sort, tree
and human rooted together
but now on the move. Note drag marks
where boughs flail as the creature
propels itself toward the village
where it will find all the shops closed.

You don't believe that people
metamorphose into trees,
but I think that trees aspire
to human angst and mobility,
muscling their roots into action
to articulate themselves awake.
Let's follow the tracks. The forest
sighs those windy little sighs
that invoke Germanic gloom
peopled with trolls and gnomes.

The creature has slipped over the brook,
past the ruined log cabin, behind
a cul-de-sac of vinyl condos,
across the town's oldest graveyard,
and down a slope of pines to Grove Street,
where we lose the tracks. Wandering,
we discover a café open
and steaming with fresh baked goods.

One man seated and snorting coffee,
his rough wool clothes all twigged and burred
and his beard a plait of brownish weed.
He rustles a newspaper and frowns.
His ordinary boots couldn't leave
those gnarled tracks we've followed,
but we want to ask him anyway
if he has ever felt like a tree.

The café owner smiles and greets us
by name, her apron starched to kill.
The fogged windows mask the world
outdoors. We order coffee and sit.
Tired from a long walk through snow,
we allow our roots to touch the floor
while our wooden thoughts toughen
against the winter still to come.

THERE AND BACK AGAIN
Heidi Schultz

Being young during the 70s, I grew up in central Pennsylvania, the oldest child of three in a traditional family. It was a time when freedom still felt like the calling card of the day. My brother, sister, and I wandered the woods, riding bikes, building forts, and running around in pajamas in the early summer evenings, catching fireflies.

Looking back, it wasn't all rainbows. My young parents, while loving, carried with them their own traumas, as we all do. This, along with the culture of the place we lived, informed how we were raised. As a shy, sensitive, serious child, I craved nurturing and attention while absorbing the emotions of everyone around me. When I was two and a half years old, my baby brother was born. He was jaundiced and extremely colicky, injecting an element of chaos into all of our lives.

Living in a patriarchal time, we organized ourselves around the needs of my father. So when my brother arrived, naturally, attention shifted away from me. I instinctively took on the good girl role, hoping to make things as easy as possible for my parents. A little over a year later, my sister was born. An unexpected pregnancy, she was a healthy, happy little girl, but still another mouth to feed, requiring attention. My parents were building a life, made more complex with each child. My father was a social worker, and money was tight.

I was fortunate to have an outlet. My maternal grandparents built a mid-century modern home in a mountain town called Ligonier right before I was born, an hour outside of Pittsburgh. We would wind down the mountainside and cross a wooden bridge spanning the brook to reach their home. With vaulted ceilings and windows overlooking the woodland, it felt like living in a fairytale. When I was seven, my parents sent me to visit them by plane, all by myself. For me, this was solid gold. With my grandparents, I not only felt the impact of nature on my soul, but also the undivided attention they paid me.

My life was uprooted after finishing fourth grade when we moved to a different part of central PA for my father's work.

Forest-laden hillsides were replaced with flat agricultural land, and the peers who liked and accepted me were left behind. It was Amish country, and even though most of the people who lived there were not Anabaptists, there was a steadfast religious tradition that most families adhered to. Conservatism and racism were both more apparent.

Right before my family moved, the Three Mile Island nuclear disaster happened within seven miles of our newly built home. My parents were traveling there to pick out kitchen cabinets when they heard of the crisis unfolding on the car radio while crossing the Susquehanna Bridge. They immediately turned around to be with our family. I don't remember much about the incident, but I'm sure the tension seeped in as they debated still making the move. I was ten years old at the time and couldn't wrap my mind around the implications of America's first nuclear meltdown. Ultimately, we did move, and I settled, uncomfortably, into my new life.

Eventually, my grandparents sold their home in Ligonier to live permanently in Pittsburgh. At that point, I was a self-involved teenager and didn't understand the impact that losing Ligonier would have on my life. But the seeds were planted, and that magical place became a touchstone.

Another outlet was playing sports, something that came naturally. This too became difficult, as I was often ill with viruses, and eventually mono, in middle and high school. I began to have arthritic issues with my knees and elbows. Massive amounts of fluid would accumulate around one or the other knee joint, taking weeks to dissipate, only to happen again a few months later. Doctors couldn't provide a definitive diagnosis, and the condition worsened over time, developing into osteoarthritis at a young age.

I encountered more personal chaos as puberty arrived. Years of stuffing my feelings, people-pleasing, and living up to my good girl image were catching up to me as my body began to cycle and change. I became even more physically and emotionally sensitive. I was an early bloomer, gaining womanly weight and developing a large chest, bringing unwanted attention. I was also young for my grade, beginning kindergarten when I was four, so while my physical development happened early, my emotional development lagged. I felt like a volcano getting closer and closer to erupting. This psychic struggle began to show up physically in my body.

I began to long for attention from boys despite my shy nature. My parents were in a beautiful, committed relationship since college, which I wished to emulate. I didn't understand that life is not like following a rule book. In my own black and white mind, I thought that meeting a man at a young age would yield the same outcome. I began to act in ways that were destructive and potentially dangerous. Some boys took advantage of this dynamic, toying with my need for intimacy, which was emotionally damaging.

I discovered alcohol during my junior year of high school and began to lose control. Drinking was the release valve that I was seeking and the stopper to my volcanic state of being. I was still doing well in school and involved in athletics, but sought out any chance I could to escape through drinking and connecting with others. Even reasonable amounts of alcohol made me ill, but the release of inhibition pulled me back to it again and again. The habit was compounded by taking ortho novum 777 as a solution for an extremely heavy cycle, now considered a very high dose birth control pill. I can only wonder how taking these potent hormones affected my physical and emotional state.

Attending college at a very large state university, there were other physical tolls, including debilitating migraines, anxiety, arthritic episodes, and depression. I graduated, majoring in Health Policy and Administration, putting me on the same professional trajectory as my father, as he was now a hospital administrator. It was the late 80s, a time of conservatism and capitalism, and I wanted to be a business woman. Years of micro traumas, manifesting in emotional dissociation, people pleasing, and binge drinking, resulted in disembodiment of my mental self, from my emotional self, from my physical self. I had no idea how to connect with my true nature and discern who I was and what life path interested me. Instead, I took cues from the surrounding culture and adopted the ambitions of the people I was closest to.

Following college graduation in '91, when jobs were hard to come by, I accepted a position as a Physician Recruiter in Pittsburgh. I hated it. Desperate to escape the situation, I was accepted into an MBA/Masters of Health Administration dual degree program at the local city University. I did relatively well despite my health challenges and party lifestyle, but upon graduation, felt lost again. I did not want to be a healthcare administrator. Instead, I took a job managing a coffee shop at a small local chain where I was a barista.

This began my jack-of-all-trades career trajectory, with each new job loosely linked to the last, but different. I worked in the admissions office at a local women's college, advising graduate health students. I then took a sales position at a tech company, selling online applications and recruitment software to colleges and universities. After being laid off, I sold power wheelchairs for a year, driving a van throughout western PA, West Virginia, and Ohio, demonstrating the chair in homes throughout the region. Some people lived in squalor, as many clients were poor, relying on Medicaid for health coverage. While I discovered empathy and value in older generations, because I was still disembodied, it became another soul sucking job. None of these jobs truly resonated.

I finally landed in the nonprofit sector as an Outreach Coordinator at CASA, an organization advocating for children who experience abuse and neglect, which was a better fit. I could relate easily with people and felt more comfortable with the work. Since then, I've worked at four other non-profits, three of which benefit children. I felt good about the work, but still wasn't feeling truly fulfilled, and it was challenging to maintain my work schedule given my variable health.

In 1998, still incessantly seeking that elusive relationship, I married a man who managed the coffee shop I worked at while in graduate school. In retrospect, the attraction made sense, as we were both somewhat lost, unable to identify who we were at our core. After two years of marriage, while working in Graduate Admissions, I felt I was beginning to find my purpose, as my spouse was still struggling to find his. My perspective was skewed, but served to extract me from a marriage that was a bad fit.

Sporadically, through it all, there would be times when my body would break down, overwhelmed with exhaustion, pain, anxiety, and depression, and I would be bedridden. In my late twenties and thirties, I began to experience pain all over my body, something that I would describe as fascial pain. My mind felt sluggish and foggy, and anxious most of the time. I was still relentlessly seeking a love relationship, thinking that finding the right match would be a panacea and support. Being a seeker and an optimist, I saw countless numbers of health specialists and therapists throughout the years, attempting to understand what was happening to my body, with no real answers. By my mid-thirties, I began to wonder if I would have the chance to have children, something that I had hoped for but was frightening, given the state of my health.

In my thirties, I met a lawyer originally from a small town in New Hampshire, not far from the Lakes Region. We visited his family there, once in the summer and once in the winter. Filled with mountains, ponds, and rivers surrounding quaint small towns, with access to the seacoast, New Hampshire had everything I was looking for. Most significantly, it had serenity. It reminded me of Ligonier, the place that imprinted on my psyche so strongly growing up.

The relationship was fraught, and we both abused our own bodies in different ways, so once again, I ended the relationship. But the residual question that nagged the edges of my mind was, "How do I get to New Hampshire?" I had fallen out of love with a person and in love with a place. A place that felt so familiar my soul felt at peace. I began researching psychology programs there but never built up the nerve to apply. I had a full-time job which I felt good about, and most of my family was in Pittsburgh, which felt safe.

Right after graduating from college, I moved in with my best friend from high school, who was finishing undergraduate studies at the local university. We lived with her boyfriend and his friend, who were in the same fraternity. I began spending time at local bars with many of their 'brothers,' drinking and socializing. One was a good-looking, thin, intelligent young man who was just my type. He and his longtime girlfriend had recently broken up, and I made my interest known to him. We spent a blissful week together, but then he stopped calling me. I was crushed. He didn't explain himself, but I later realized that he planned a move to Colorado and that the intensity with which I pursued a relationship most likely put him off.

In 2006, the same band of fraternity brothers planned a reunion, and I finagled my way into attending. My secret wish was to see if my former crush was in attendance. He was, and when I had the chance to speak with him, I couldn't believe my good fortune. He was single AND living in New Hampshire. Afterward, I sent him a postcard explaining how nice it was to see him and gave him my contact information. He got in touch when he was back in Pittsburgh visiting family, and we began dating long-distance. It was difficult. We weren't a natural match, and once again, after many months, he broke it off. I was devastated. I was almost 37 years old, and the possibility of having children was beginning to wane. Several months later, I called and left him a voice message, saying hello on his birthday. Little did I know that day, he had an MRI for a worsening vision issue. The call intersected with the circumstance and touched him, and we resumed our relationship.

I moved to New Hampshire the summer of 2007 to give the relationship a real try, and we planned to marry despite tensions and strain. I became pregnant with our son two months before the wedding, who was born just before I turned forty. Our marriage was complex, and living together proved difficult. I had moved to Southwestern NH, in the Monadnock region, where neither of us knew a single person, despite him living there for several years prior. But I had somehow wandered back to a place rooted in the seat of my soul, a place that mimicked my childhood refuge.

Our son was born healthy, but the connection with my husband continued to deteriorate. I struggled to find work, and the strain of parenting and living together was taking a toll. The health issues that began in my childhood expanded after the birth of our son. Further testing revealed that at some point in my life, I contracted Lyme disease and at least one other tick-borne infection. I spent six grueling years treating this and other health issues, including Epstein Barr virus, strep throat, giardia, chronic fatigue, joint and fascial pain, and more. Over time, I realized that my husband and I should separate as the tensions between us increased. After ten years of marriage, I moved into an apartment a mile from our home.

While recovering from the grief of yet another failed relationship, I began to understand that being here in New Hampshire was not about a person but about a place. I was back in a refuge of natural safety and security, where I could reconnect to the authentic self that fractured all those years ago. After years of therapy, use of antidepressants, and fiercely seeking reasons for my myriad health issues, I joined a therapeutic group of women. We explored how to recognize trauma, learning tools, and practices of healing in a judgment free setting. I began to connect my body, mind, and emotions after decades of compartmentalizing them into separate entities.

For the first time, I felt connected to my feelings by dialing into my own knowing and intuition. I started using them as my guide. I rediscovered my values instead of usurping them from others. I began to dream, explore, and write, allowing curiosity to lead me to the next right thing in life. I recognized that I was already whole as I listened to my inner voice instead of seeking answers from the world at large. While this continuing work has not resolved all my health issues, they are no longer exacerbated by fear, anxiety, and depression.

I am learning to regulate my nervous system and am healing my body by living a life of authenticity. The seeds of integrity already existed inside of that pre-fractured girl. The roots that grew in Ligonier, where I experienced nature and nurture spread, leading me to New Hampshire, back home, and back to myself.

"KINTSUGI"

Bradley A. Michalsson

Fill with gold your fault lines–
the scars of error, and
forked paths pursued to failure.
Let the molten ore firm up
the spider-webbing tumble.
Allow it to settle into the low points,
your valleys of choice and outcome.
And think of it not as blemish, nor
evidence of a life so carelessly lived,
but a testament to perseverance,
a way to rise above the ash of before.

What is strength?
Not a pillar, or a beacon upon a hill. No.
They are too easily built to be icons
with no substance, loans with no collateral.
Observe the folly: the obsidian monolith,
seemingly stalwart, worn by wind and rain,
will cleave into fragments with strain.

It is simply a gathering of the shards,
a shoring up of the walls–all gluing,
and a patchwork and oaken beams bracing
against what was previously torn asunder.

Because everyone falls apart sometimes–
that of itself should not be the heels
that remained undipped.
So let the cracks be not a reminder
that you once were broken,
but a declaration that you found within
something precious and the ability to mend.

"COVERED BRIDGE"
WILLIAM BELISLE

Our Contributors

ABOUT OUR PRESIDENT

Steven Michaels is the author of *Sweet Life of Mystery*, a parody of the whodunit genre. He has been featured on The Satirist website for his scintillating take on current affairs, and has written, produced, and directed over twenty plays for students at Winchester School in New Hampshire. Steve co-founded the Quabbin Quills in 2017 and was instrumental in creating the first anthology, *Time's Reservoir* and he hopes you have enjoyed the work he has featured in all of Quabbin Quills' anthologies. He is also very thankful to all the authors who have come to share his writer's dream.

ABOUT OUR PUBLISHER

Garrett Zecker is the publisher and co-founder of Quabbin Quills. He holds an MA in English from Fitchburg State University and an MFA in Fiction from Southern New Hampshire University's Mountainview MFA. He founded Perpetual Imagination in 2004, specializing in independent releases and live events. Garrett is a writer, actor, and teacher of writing and literature. Links to his work, including other publications, full Shakespeare In The Park performances, and hundreds of book and movie reviews can be found at his blog, GarrettZecker.com.

ABOUT OUR EDITORS

Cecilia Januszewski has a BA in linguistic anthropology from Reed College, and currently lives in the Bay Area. She has worked on the editorial boards of multiple literary and academic journals, including *Radicle*, *Manuscripts*, and, of course, *Quabbin Quills*. She has published several short stories and poems and looks forward to publishing many more (just don't ask about her novel, which she's been working on forever and still hasn't quite finished).

Chele Pedersen Smith lives in Ashburnham, Massachusetts with her husband Bob, who just shakes his head at her crazy ideas. They recently adopted two bonded golden retrievers named Trixie and Kendra-Betsy. Chele (short for Michele), is a pharmacy technician at Hannaford and a mom to two grown kids and two grand-bunnies. She became an "Editor at Large" for Quabbin Quills in 2024. Besides having a spiritual short published in *Guideposts* magazine in 2019, Chele has a recurring humor-in-life column in the free New Zealand digital magazine, *Inflow*. She also has nine published varied-genre mystery-comedies and is thrilled to have stories in three previous Quabbin Quill's anthologies. Her array of mysteries can be found at The Book Forge in Orange, Creative Connections Gift Shop in Ashburnham, and on her Amazon author page.

Charlotte Taylor has published short stories and poetry and hoards a collection of unedited novels. She loves the process of creating characters, stories, and worlds. Charlotte is an active blogger for her work in Ayurveda medicine and yoga. She is actively seeking a life of peace, study, and fun. Charlotte can often be found surrounded by cats while she sips tea and reads books. Other times, you'll find her practicing yoga, climbing mountains, and sometimes crawling under barbed wire.

Diane Hinckley describes herself as a perpetually baffled individual who likes to make up stories.

Author **Diane Kane** is one of the founding members of Quabbin Quill's non-profit writers' group. Kane recently released her debut novel, *I Never Called Him Pa*. Her short stories appear in several Red Penguin Publications, including her winning historical fiction piece, "Ernest Lived." She also has multiple stories in *Monadnock Underground* print anthologies and their online magazine. She is the publisher and co-author of *Flash in the Can Number One* and *Number Two*, which contain short stories to read wherever you go. In addition, Kane writes public interest articles for *Uniquely Quabbin Magazine* and local newspapers, as well as professional reviews for *Readers' Favorite*. Kane's first children's book, *Don Gateau the Three-Legged Cat of Seborga,* published in English, Spanish, French and Italian, won the Purple Dragonfly Award for illustrations and Caring/Making a Difference in 2020. Her second children's book, *Brayden the Brave Goes to the Hospital*, published April 2021 and endorsed by Boston Children's Hospital, is helping children and families in children's hospitals across the country.

Fred Gerhard is an editor for Quabbin Quills anthologies, and for *Smoky Quartz – an Online Journal of Literature and Art.* His poems have appeared in numerous magazines. His books include *Drifting to "Hello"* (Khotso Publishing, 2023) and the chapbook *Lilacs Still Bloom in Ashburnham: Songs of Spring* (Local Gems Poetry Press, 2023). A winner of the 2023 Poetry in the Pines Contest, his work is displayed at Cathedral in the Pines in Rindge, NH. He is a founder of the New Dawn Writers' Group where he leads monthly poetry workshops. He enjoys spending time on his porch in the company of friends and a surprisingly agile tortoise named Twylah.

James Thibeault is the Treasurer and a dedicated board member of Quabbin Quills. He currently works as a librarian at Bentley University. Search for his novels, *Deacon's Folly* and *Michael's Black Dress*, in bookstores, as well as his children's book, *Melanie and the Box.*

Kathy Chencharik is a freelance writer and has been published in several newspapers, magazines, and anthologies. She won the Derringer Award for best flash fiction for her short story, "The Book Signing " in *Thin Ice* (a Level Best Books anthology, 2010). She earned numerous honorable mentions for her stories in *Alfred Hitchcock's Mystery Magazine*'s Mysterious Photograph contest. Her story "the Widow " finally won the prize in the November/December 2020 issue of the magazine.

Michael Young is the current Poet Laureate for Royalston, MA. His work has appeared in three former Quabbin Quills anthologies, *Uniquely Quabbin Magazine,* and three publications: *Trout, Grit,* and *A Time for Singing.* Currently he is working on his memoir, *Playing in the Weeds.* An Adult Education instructor in creative writing at MWCC (The Mount), two of his students have pieces in *Beyond the Pathway.* Michael enjoys fly fishing when not writing or working with his wife, Pat, on their Greenfyre Farm. His weekly *Universal Meditation* show may be heard on WVAO-FM.

Sharon A. Harmon is a poet and freelance writer. Her chapbooks are *Swimming with Cats* and *Wishbone in a Lightning Jar.* She is the author of two children's books. She has published over 300 poems and also writes for magazines and anthologies. She has been published twice in *Chicken Soup for the Soul*, as well as *Taste of Home, Birds and Blooms,* and *Highlights for Children.* Her poetry has appeared in *The Paterson Literary Review*, *Writing the Land Northeast,* and *Compass Roads.* Sharon has taught workshops for writing poetry, memoir, and writing for magazines. Find her on Facebook at Sharon A. Harmon Poet & Writer and also Sharon Ann Harmon Publishing.

OUR STUDENT SCHOLARSHIP CONTRIBUTORS

Moss Maloney is a lover of poetry. Moss started to enter contests to let their work out into the world. Moss loves the written word and also is a part of a Choral group.

Via Rose loves writing and singing. Her dream is to one day create movies and shows that tell stories that have never been heard of. Her favorite movie is *Alice in Wonderland*. Her favorite color is periwinkle blue. She has two dogs Gracie and Max, both German Shepard, and a grey tabby cat, named tiger. She loves writing poems, for it is her form of emotion and expression.

Kassandra Santos has grown up in a small town in Massachusetts, living there her entire life. She is 17 years old and likes to think she is a decent writer/poet. Last year, in November, she won a poetry writing contest at her local library. There was no prompt and everyone had different genres of poems. She plays softball as a pitcher for her high school team, and her sister is the catcher. Her English teacher is the softball coach, and she has inspired me to take the modern poetry class and write more.

Alex Murdock is 18 years old and lives in the nice small and quiet town of Winchendon. He often likes to spend his time playing games but he tries his best to find time to play with friends, as he gets bored of playing alone. He also likes to watch Youtube videos ranging from "How to's" to gameplay on some of his favorite games. He also likes a few smaller things such as the color blue, Chinese buffets, and being at home.He often loves playing Minecraft, Geometry Dash, Fortnite, and Genshin Impact. He also enjoys a wonderful Shirley Temple and Charleston Chews or KitKats. He definitely has been known and describe as, hard to believe or not a very smart and talented person, along with being sometimes funny, great to be around, and overall a good friend. Although he is not often seen helping around, it is very well and much appreciated when he does help. He strives to become a great and well known Youtuber with a side hobby of helping repair others' computers, laptops, and phones.

Jayden Lindsay is a student at Murdock high school who was first published in our previous anthology, *Our Wild Winds*. She has a great deal of writing experience via school and personal work. She loves writing poetry, stories, reading, and drawing. She is an only child and has two lovely dogs.

ABOUT OUR CONTRIBUTORS

Alison Clark is an aspiring poet who enjoys writing in her free time. Her main inspirations are nature, sunsets, and often the moon. This is her third publication in a Quabbin Quills anthology.

Aurynanya writes dark and devastating poetry, invoking the raw, honest, and beautifully tragic soul from her home in Massachusetts. Her work has appeared in *Hellbound Books*, *Hearth & Coffin, Move Me Poetry,* and more. Aury published the limited edition *Between Blood and Bone* dark poetry collection in 2022. *My Heart is Out for Blood* is her recent collection, published by Castle Carrington Publishing. When her spoiled black cats allow, she is also an editor and local performer. Find her at: www.aurynanya.com

Allan Fournier is a retired software engineer who has always enjoyed working with words. He enjoys sharing his poems at local poetry and open mic nights, and appeared in the *Beyond the Pathway* and *Our Wild Winds* Quabbin Quills anthologies

This is **Barbara Vosburgh's** third time in our anthology. Barbara lives in Fitchburg with her daughter, son-in-law, and grandson, who all keep her very busy. She has lived in eight states and the Marshall Islands writing all along the way. Her hobbies include gardening, knitting, reading, writing, crafting, and holiday cookie baking. She has a degree in computer programming and systems analysis. In her former life she was a news reporter, feature and humor writer. Retired now, she daily feeds a group of wild critters outside, and is working on a children's book about her squirrels. Other critters include rabbits, chipmunks, turkeys, a variety of birds and occasionally a fox, opossum, and racoons. She is recovering from an injury she got when trying to save a chipmunk from a wayward heron. Barbara is honored to be among such talented writers and has become friends with many.

Bradley A. Michalsson lives in the North Quabbin region of Massachusetts and is a writer of fiction and poetry. He has a degree in film and writing from Keene State College and began his career writing online articles about goings-on in the Tewksbury and Chelmsford, MA areas. He is currently working on a crime fiction novel that he hopes to publish in the next year. Bradley lives with his wife and two sons, one dog, and sixteen chickens. He enjoys running the trails nearby his house and living amongst nature. He paints and disc golfs in his leisure time.

Cathy Carlton Hews recently performed in NYC in a play called, *The Dog Show*. She is completing her second book, *The Little Wanderer: The Effects of Childhood Trauma*. Her first was a memoir about care-taking for a parent with Alzheimer's titled, *A Bagful of Kittens Headed to the Lake*. One of the essays, "I'm Seeing a Bunch of Bitches Later," won an honorable mention in *Writer's Digest* annual writing contest – memoir category. She has written for Stage Raw, a Los Angeles theater website. She also had a weekly column,"Backstage with Betty" in *Eye Spy L.A*, from 2005 to 2007.

Catherine Reed has been the featured poet at area poetry readings for many years. Reed also served on the WCPA's board of directors. *SAHARA, Dark Horse, Ballard Street Poetry Journal, The Purple*, and *Windfall* have published her poetry. She won the Barbara Pilon Poetry Contest and Dark Horse Third World contest, and is the author of four books of poetry: *Crossing Boundaries, Between Midnight and Dawn, Sankofa*, and *Fire Goes Out Without Wood*. She is the host of WCCA-TV's *A Journey of Words*, and a graduate of Clark University in Worcester, MA, Kaleo School of Ministry in Woburn, MA, Hartford Seminary BMCP in Hartford, CT, Brigham and Women's Chaplaincy Program, and she has attended Boston University School of Theology. She is an Associate Pastor of John Street Baptist Church of Worcester and a retired Protestant Chaplain of The College of the Holy Cross.

Clare Green of Warwick is an author, column writer for the *Uniquely Quabbin* magazine and an educator. She has been clairvoyant since childhood. She offers her insights silently, or verbally when asked. Clare welcomes folks to enjoy a cup of tea while visiting her fairy cottage or walking the backyard woodland labyrinth for peace and reflection. www.claregreenbooks.com

Clare Kirkwood is a former chef and Army veteran. Her work has been published in *Uniquely Quabbin*, Quabbin Quill's *Time's Reservoir, Reminiscence Magazine*, and *Porsche 356 Registry*.

David Story Allen's published works include *Off Tom Nevers (*2017) and *Minot's Ledge* (2023); both novels are set at a New England boarding school. In addition to having worked at such institutions, he has taught in Japan and South Korea and holds degrees from Harvard, the University of New Hampshire, and Syracuse. He teaches in New Hampshire and Massachusetts.

Debbie Patryn lives in Southwick, Massachusetts. She has stories frequently published in *Southwoods Magazine*, a monthly magazine published in Southwick.She has also had a story published in the *Westfield State University Alumni* magazine.

Ed Ahern resumed writing after forty odd years in foreign intelligence and international sales. He's had over 450 stories and poems published so far, and ten books. Ed works the other side of writing at *Bewildering Stories* where he manages a posse of eight review editors, and as lead editor at *Scribes Microfiction.* Visit these websites for more info; @bottomstripper on Twitter, @EdAhern73 on Facebook, and @edwardahern1860 on Instagram.

Eileen Hernandez-Cole ramped up her writing after attending a Boston Writing Workshop a few years ago. By day, Eileen works in IT and lives surrounded by the scenic hills and hiking trails of Central Massachusetts with her husband and children.

Elaine Reardon is a writer, educator, and artist. Her first chapbook, *The Heart is a Nursery For Hope*, won first honors from Flutter Press in 2016. Her second chapbook, *Look Behind You*, was also published by Flutter Press. Finishing Line Press is publishing her third chapbook soon. For more go to: www.elainereardon.wordpress.com.

Eliza Murphy resides in southern Maine with her husband and her cat Cornelia. She is an amateur historian, aspiring novelist, and sometimes a poet. Her 2023 debut novel, *Forget Everything and Run* is available on Amazon. You can find her at ElizaMurphy-author on Facebook and Instagram.

Elaine Daisy McKay resides in Hubbardston, MA with her husband, Donald. They are the retired owners, after 32 years, of Calico & Creme, a well-known restaurant and home-made ice cream shop, which they built right there on their farm. Having a creative mind, Elaine has always loved to look for the simplicity of life, taking a picture, sketching, or writing about it. Now she has the joy of passing on these written legacies to her granddaughter, Erin. "The Old Cellar Door " prose poem has a special place in her heart, as it involves her precious grandchildren. Elaine also remembers being measured as a child by her dad on their old cellar door back in the early 40's. Her granddaughter, Erin Morrissey, has been helping her gather the many stories that Elaine has written over her lifetime. The poem included in this anthology is one of Erin's favorites.

Heidi Larsen is a fourth-grade teacher at a small Christian Academy in Central Massachusetts. She is a storyteller and writer at heart, who uses her Masters in Education to make words come to life. Her work appears in the Quabbin Quills Anthology 2023 and has been featured at the New Dawn Arts Center and Creative Connections Gift & Gallery in Ashburnham.

Heidi Schultz is an existential explorer. Never quite fitting in, she finds refuge in words, through books, journaling, and even some poetry writing, and in the beauty and expansiveness of nature. Always a seeker and growth-oriented person, she has a massive curiosity about people and the world that we live in. Her failures have provided fertile ground for shedding old ways of being. She leans into vulnerability and authenticity, which aids in finding her voice and path in the process. You can find Heidi on Instagram

@notrunofthemill.curations and on her blog at notrunofthemill.wordpress.com

J. A. McIntosh, a recovering attorney, writes the Meredith, Massachusetts mystery series about imperfect people seeking justice. Her latest novel, *Swift River Secrets*, is due to be published in 2024. She is the president of the Swift River Valley Historical Society.

James Wyman is the last full-time resident on a one-lane, dirt, dead-end road at the tip of a long peninsula in the middle of a very large lake in northern Vermont. He was born and raised in the foothills of the Longfellow Range of the Appalachian Mountains in western Maine. Never having lived more than 50 miles from 45 degrees north latitude, he has grown to appreciate the texture of the woods, fields, and hills of New England, and the myriad of colors—ranging from the cold black and white of winter to the light-filled prism of a hardwood forest in fall. Jim's photography reflects nature's beauty and the human condition. Jim teaches at the Community College of Vermont. His photography has been published in "Defunkt Magazine." His poetry has been published in "Maya's Review: The Closed Eye Open," and will appear in the March 2024 edition of "Ink In Thirds." He is the author of "Picture Perfect Poems"

Janet Bowdan's poems have appeared in *APR*, *Tahoma Literary Review*, The Rewilding Anthology, *Sequestrum*, *Lit Shark*, and elsewhere. As the editor of *Common Ground Review*, she grew up in South Hadley (where "Pop" is set).

Jessica Dawson, a life-long New Englander, can't bear to part from its beauty. This love for home inspires her to incorporate the natural world into her poetry, creating characters out of the flora and fauna that Northeast natives revere.

Jim Metcalf began an enjoyable hobby of writing short stories for various media following a business career that included writing memos, proposals, reports, and newsletters. His wife of 55 years died unexpectedly, casting him into deep grief. A friend in a grief group suggested that he write a short paragraph about, "The love of his life." It was therapeutic, and a writer suggested expanding the paragraph to a memoir titled, *A One-Sided Coin*. Jim is now writing a collection of stories entitled, *Flavors of Maine*.

Jon Bishop is an MFA candidate at the University of St. Thomas, where he studies poetry. His work has appeared in a wide variety of outlets.

Joseph E. Lorion served in the U S Navy 1967-1973. He is a retired railroad worker after 34 years. Lorion has been fishing and hunting since he was four years old. He is a member of the Fish and Game Committee of the Royalston Fish and Game Club. He and his wife, Robin, have lived in Phillipston since 1993.

Karen Traub is a library-loving, local history buff and belly dancer. She holds an MFA in creative writing from Salve Regina University and has written for *Brevity Blog*, *Multiplicity Magazine*, and Quabbin Quills anthologies. https://www.clippings.me/users/happydancermom

Karen Wagner, a physicist, writes poetry as a retirement vocation. Her work appears in the Quabbin Quills Anthology, the Goose River Anthology and the *BOLLI Journal*. She enjoys wordsmithing and expression of concepts beyond the realm of logic. Although she prefers to write about rabbits who find the garden gate and the sand-blown purple sky of Morocco, she tuned her work down a bit for this edition of the *Quabbin Quills*. Karen lives in Hudson, MA with her cat, Star.

Kathryn Chaisson dedicates her piece to her late father, reporter and historian Richard J. Chaisson who always encouraged and supported her love for writing.

Kersti Slowik has written advertorials, newsletters, and web content, but her first love is writing relatable, greeting card-style poetry. A graduate of Northeastern University, she was previously published in two Quabbin Quills anthologies. Kersti loves musical theater and enjoys seeing shows with her family both locally and on Broadway. She lives with her husband and daughter outside of Boston. She can be reached at kerstiiswriting.com.

Kimberly Beckham is a wanderer, photographer, reader, writer, hopeful lady with two old demanding cats and a love of wandering with no plan, breakfast cereal and lego building.

Larry Barrieau is a New Englander, born and raised in Gardner, Massachusetts. A Navy veteran, he traveled extensively across the country, finally settling back in Massachusetts where he raised his sons and taught middle-school for over thirty years. Now retired, he is writing his memoirs of his many adventures. His writing has been published in *Accenti* magazine and has won awards at the Hardwick Fair. He is married and has two wonderful grandsons.

Laurie Rosen is a lifelong New Englander. Her poetry has appeared in *Peregrine, Gyroscope Review, Zig Zag* lit mag, *New Verse News*, *Oddball Magazine*, *The Inquisitive Eater*: a journal of The New School, *One Art,* and elsewhere. Laurie won first place in poetry at the 2023 Marblehead, MA Festival of the Arts.

Les Clark, an author of four books, thought he could retire and watch TCM all day but it's not to be. He's back to work at Staples one day a week, restaurant hopping with Irene, and planning a trip to the Air Force Museum in Ohio. Beside contributing to *Quabbin Quills*, Les' latest book is titled, *Inside The Darkside*: 12 short science fiction stories of time travel, first contact, dating sites and other genres. He is a USAF veteran, grew up in Boston and toiled seventeen years at night getting degrees at Northeastern. His favorite mode of travel is an easy chair.

Lisa Lindstromm has penned multiple retirement skits and parodies for dear and forgiving friends, published a few business articles and jotted down travel notes on both sides of the pond. She then decided it was high time to dust off her pen and see what becomes of it.

Lorri Ventura is a retired special education administrator living in Massachusetts. Her poems have been featured in a number of publications. She is a three-time winner of *Writing in a Woman's Voice's* Moon Prize award for poetry.

LuAnn Thibodeau writes a monthly article for *Worcester Pulse Magazine* and in the past year, has written articles as well as the cover stories for its sister publication- *CM Pride*. In addition, LuAnn wrote an article for *Boston Spirit Magazine* about the local young lady from Fitchburg who was a finalist in last season's *America's Got Talent*. She writes regularly on social media, with many odes and more to friends and others. LuAnn is currently writing two books: one about her travel adventures, and another about the spirits who inhabit The SK Pierce Haunted Mansion in Gardner, where she is part of the tour guide team.

Mackenzie Scanlon is a writer who enjoys writing poetry. She has a Bachelor's degree in Business Management from Bridgewater State University. Her work has also been included in the Quabbin Quills anthology *Our Wild Winds*.

Marilynn Carter is a holistic health practitioner, teacher and life coach at Many Paths for Health; co-owner of Maat Publishing; and author of two books, *No Fret Cooking*, and *Experience the Love Light Wisdom of Reiki*. Her poetry has appeared in *Trouvaille Review;* the Merrimac Mic Anthology II: *Going with the Floes; Lunation*, *A Good Fat* Anthology of 114 Women Poets; and *Klarissa Dreams Redux: The Illuminated Anthology*; at the Methuen Arts outdoor poetry installation, *Words by Winter Waterfall*; *Word Play*, a virtual exhibit of poetic art. Her first chapbook of poetry was published in 2021.

Mary Anne Kalonas Slack's debut novel, *The Sacrificial Daughter* was released in February, 2024. Her stories have appeared in *MUSED*, *Adelaide Literary Magazine*, and in the 2023 Quabbin Quills anthology, *Our Wild Winds*. Visit maryanneslack.com for more information.

Molly Chambers is a retired social worker who lives in Greenfield,Ma. She remembers Sundays in Chester, PA where she was actively involved in the Civil Rights Movement.

Phyllis Cochran started writing in 1990 after retiring from a business career. Her stories have appeared in *Woman's World, Chicken Soup for the Soul, Focus on the Family, Decision Magazine* and many more including national and international magazines. Her first book, *Shades of Light: A Mother and Daughter's Pathway to God* was published in 2006. She finds joy in attending women's Bible studies and spending time with her great grandchildren, teaching them how to write.

This is **Quinley Sologaistoa's** first ever publication but writing has always been a passion of hers. She looks forward to now calling herself a published author! Yet she humbly remains a bird loving, hobby writing college student.

Stacy Boone returned to the east coast after living in southwest Colorado for a decade. Spending as much time outside as possible allows her to witness a landscape that is radically changing. As a backpacking guide she shared with others how to build their own outdoor relationship. Now, she writes, mostly about water. Her most recent stories can be found in *Appalachia Journal* and *The Upper New Review.*

Sue Moreines is a retired child psychologist who enjoys writing short stories, supporting non-profit organizations, and paying-it-forward. Sue and her rescue dog, Daisy, volunteer at the library to allow young children the opportunity to practice reading and enjoy the benefits of pet therapy.

Dr. Thomas Reed Willemain is an academic, software entrepreneur and former intelligence officer. His flash fiction has twice been nominated for a Pushcart Prize and has appeared in *Granfalloon, Hobart,* Quabbin Quills, and elsewhere. He holds degrees from Princeton University and Massachusetts Institute of Technology. He and his wife recently moved into a senior living community in his hometown of South Hadley, MA.

Tom Anthony is a retired college administrator now living in Maine. Besides writing in multiple genres, current interests include cycling, wood carving, cabinetry, opera, medieval history, foreign travel, and current affairs.

William Belisle is a retired technical writer now enjoying more creative writing.

William Doreski lives in Peterborough, New Hampshire. He has taught at several colleges and universities. His most recent book of poetry is *Venus, Jupiter* (2023). His essays, poetry, fiction, and reviews have appeared in many journals.

Support Our Local Sponsors!

Printing yearly anthologies isn't cheap.

Thankfully, Quabbin Quills has some wonderful local sponsors to help with production costs, so please consider reaching out and supporting them!

This anthology has been brought to you by the following generous sponsors ...

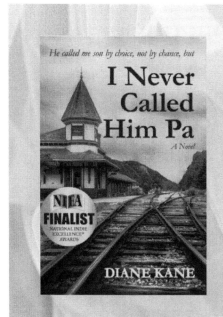

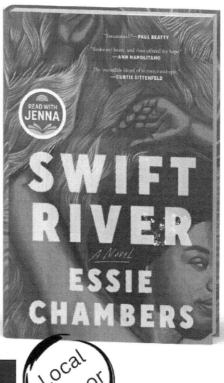

When a mother's love becomes a daughter's burden, is there really a way out?

THE
SACRIFICIAL
DAUGHTER
Mary Anne Kalonas Slack

Adventure and Romance, with all the facets of a complicated mother-daughter relationship

ELAINE REARDON

STORIES TOLD
in a LOST TONGUE

Elaine Reardon

PROUDLY PRESENTED BY
FINISHING LINE PRESS

Reardon's stovetops and herb gardens ultimately serve up comfort and hope: each meticulously crafted poem offers "a newly hatched bird" as we wait expectantly for "bits of sweetness to fall." These poems are a reminder of our cravings for home, dreams of reclaiming lost languages and holding them in our mouths now, and our insatiable hunger for poetry this alive.— Casey Jarrin, Ph.D. | Poet & Educator

https://www.finishinglinepress.com/product /stories-told-in-a-lost-tongue-by-elaine- reardon/

Corner Cafe

Fresh baked goods daily, Deans Beans coffee, Soups, Sandwiches, Hot Meals. Take Out and Inside Dining!
Order online, in house, or call ahead!

1 S Main St, Orange, MA
(978) 633-4433

PART OUTFITTER, PART GENERAL STORE AND PART OF THE BEAUTIFUL NORTH QUABBIN!

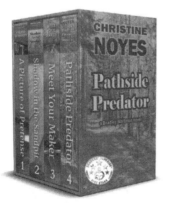

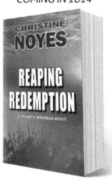

SWIFT RIVER SECRETS

A NEW MYSTERY BY J. A. MCINTOSH

A modern day murder at an historical society.
Animosities that go back a century. A mystery of the
Quabbin Reservoir

COMING SEPT. 2024

WITTY'S

FUNERAL HOME

158 South Main Street
Orange, MA 01364-0133
978-544-3160
wittyfuneralhome.com

New from Khotso Publishing

DRIFTING TO "HELLO"

Poems by
Fred Gerhard

"These poems tap gently at our door and invite us to join
the dance of dandelions and red catkins, bobcats and
trolleys, of life and death and love." —**Barbara
Morrison**, author of *Terrarium* and *Here at Least*

Available at FredGerhard.com

269

CONGRATULATIONS
AUTHORS, EDITORS &
PUBLISHER
OF QUABBIN QUILLS'
7TH ANTHOLOGY,
WANDERING ROOTS!

FROM
JIM METCALF

"ROOT MAN"
DIANE KANE

Made in the USA
Middletown, DE
29 August 2024

59840309R00157